Olivia Holmes
Has Inherited
A Vineyard

MARK DAYDY

Cover design by MIKE DAYDY

CONTENTS

1

Don't Panic! It's Only a Weekend of Stress, Anxiety & Humiliation

Forty-four-year-old Olivia Holmes wished to be anywhere but the magnificent lobby of the 300-year-old Raglington Hall Hotel on England's South Downs. It was a vista of tasteful, muted greens and yellows with superb oil paintings – rural landscapes and family portraits – hung between giant cheese plants in huge terracotta pots. In short, stunning. If only she hadn't been forced there for a weekend of corporate team building.

Olivia hated company get-togethers, but as one of thirty-five Prior Grove employees, she had no say in the matter. Especially this year when the London-based public relations firm was struggling to attract enough work.

In the light of possible restructuring, there were already whispers about her role coming under pressure. Of course, there was no way she could stand by and let her job vanish. It had too much going for it. The monthly salary, the… the… monthly salary…

Her phone rang. It was that number again. She rejected the call. Last time, they left a voicemail, which she terminated after just a few seconds. It was someone from a law firm trying to reach her, no doubt about the minor collision in Sainsbury's car park. That other vehicle wasn't a car; it was a tank. That's all you needed – a tank driver with a lawyer.

"Could I have your attention, please?" bellowed Henry Coyle, her boss. He was three steps up on the grand staircase, looking like a rep from Vacuous Vacations. "As you know, this weekend we'll be assessing our talent pool… and can I say what amazing talent we have! Now, with possible job cuts, the directors have insisted we work hard to identify and retain our best staff and I applaud that climate of fair play."

Indeed, Henry did just that, slapping his hands together like two dead fish. Everyone grudgingly joined in.

As he launched into a familiar corporate theme, Olivia surreptitiously checked her make-up in a large, gilt-framed mirror. Maybe the youthful ponytail look wasn't doing it for her anymore. Her auburn locks showed strands of silver. Her hazel eyes, once bright, were now permanently tired. Her round face, a little fuller…

She switched her attention to a portrait hanging alongside the mirror. Sir George Raglington (1799-1864), a walrus of a man in a ceremonial crimson army uniform. A plaque listed battles he'd overseen and described his hands-on approach to the gardens here at Raglington Hall. It was, in fact, one of a series of family portraits. Next along was Sir Edward Raglington (1827-1887), a pale, bulbous individual who…

"Olivia?" said Henry, breaking off from addressing the

crowd. "Are you with us?"

Olivia turned and gave Henry her super-focused look.

"Okay," he said, "as the weather's fine, we'll be outside for much of the day. If you're not wearing footwear suitable for walking in the countryside, please go and change now. Our transport will be here shortly."

When it came to outdoor versus indoor team-building initiatives, Olivia found them equally terrible. There really wasn't much to choose between spending a rainy day trapped in a room performing embarrassing dance routines, squirting soda into people's mouths, and watching videos about the leadership structure used by chimpanzees... or spending a dry day outside re-enacting the Battle of the Somme.

But no – that was being negative. In the current climate, she needed to get stuck in. Hadn't she once been one of the go-go-girls? That was the name co-workers had given her and two other women who joined Prior Grove in the same week ten years ago. Olivia, Jools and Kimmy – fighters and do-ers. The go-go-girls. Except Jools and Kimmy had since left to start their own public relations companies. For a time, there was talk of Olivia doing likewise, and the adrenalin had certainly made her giddy with excitement – but risk wasn't something she was comfortable with. Maybe it was the super-hard work she knew Jools and Kimmy were putting in. Maybe it was memories of her father struggling to run his failing used car business and taking his own life when the debt mountain blocked out the sun.

Ten minutes later, having donned comfy converse trainers to go with her black jeans and mid-thickness crimson pullover, Olivia stood outside a building so grand she half-expected the cast of Downton Abbey to appear. On such a fine morning, with blue skies and temperatures more typical of September than November, the sunlight hitting the red brick façade seemed to set the structure ablaze.

And then there were the views. Indeed, when Olivia looked beyond the side garden, where Henry had spent most of the previous evening drooling over Clara from IT, she got a view of the distant Chilbury Folly, set among trees across the valley. This was all far too lovely to waste on a corporate weekend. It was more a place to bring a partner and spend a few days holding hands and strolling. Not that Gerry was into strolling. It wouldn't have been Alistair's thing either. He hated the countryside.

Twenty-something co-worker Rob nudged her.

"I still can't believe management didn't pay for our drinks last night. My wallet took a right kicking."

Olivia said nothing. If jobs were being cut, Rob would be a rival. Twenty years her junior, she saw only a shark scenting blood.

"Are we ready to show what we're capable of?" said Henry to those gathered.

The response was subdued.

While Henry launched into a monologue, Olivia stared across the road to the Raglington Arms pub, which did indeed display the Raglington family's coat of arms on a large sign: a shield split into four quarters, with a castle top left, a bow and arrow top right...

Family...

Olivia had no family that she knew of, and those that had gone before her certainly never qualified for a coat of arms. But if they had? A used car to represent her dad? A mop and bucket to represent her dear departed mum's long years as an NHS cleaner? And a cabbage to represent her long dead greengrocer grandfather?

A distant rumble interrupted her thoughts. Their transport was coming into view – a reassigned single decker maroon bus, which was no doubt a big saving over an executive road-cruiser. With Henry still talking, Olivia reminded herself to avoid boarding until he'd chosen his seat.

A few moments later, as Olivia and her colleagues stepped aboard, the driver welcomed them.

"Corporate weekend, is it?"

"Team-building and training," said middle-aged dyed blonde divorcee Zara in a world-weary tone that was at odds with her nuclear yellow leisure top.

"Sounds fun," said the driver. "Hopefully, you won't be too ambitious in the wilds. Last week we had the air ambulance flying a couple of dimwit office workers to hospital."

Olivia had a mini panic attack that wasn't eased by the prospect of ticking off 'helicopter ride' from her bucket list.

"Okay, everyone," said Henry, arms aloft at the rear of the bus, "today we'll be spending our time in the countryside!"

Olivia wasn't impressed. Yes, she loved the countryside, but this would be different. Whatever challenge Henry had lined up would involve sweat and pain and mud. No doubt about it.

"Are we raring to go?" Henry called.

Raring to go home, yes.

"And are we ready to work together? Because teamwork will be key as management observes you showing your true spirit in a challenge I can now reveal as… orienteering!"

Olivia tensed up.

Orien-what?

Rob nudged her. "I can name half a dozen people who will die."

2

Shine Like A Blazing Star

Following a short, stuffy bus ride, they alighted beside the folly Olivia had seen from the hotel – a whimsical Victorian waste of money designed to look like an imposing Norman cathedral from a distance, but, in reality, little more than a half-size front edifice surrounded by dwarf trees.

"Okay, everyone," said Henry, arms aloft. "Welcome to Chilbury Folly."

Olivia didn't want to spend a single minute doing orienteering – whatever the hell it was. Actually, wasn't it like mountaineering? She could see it now – Olivia Holmes, trapped on a hillside, the tricky helicopter rescue, the TV news story…

It made her feel like getting another job – except she'd already tried and failed a number of times.

"Could I have a couple of volunteers?" Henry asked.

All those who held any hope of staying with the company raised a hand, including Olivia who was aware of being watched by senior managers Scott Reece and

Charlotte Holberg.

"Excellent," said Henry. "Um… at random… how about Rob and Olivia. A round of applause for our volunteers, please."

Amid the clapping, Olivia sensed relief from those not chosen.

"Okay," said Henry. "Olivia? Perhaps you could explain to these nitwits what orienteering might involve?"

Oh Henry, you absolute ratbag…

Olivia beheld the gathering. At least fifty percent of the faces staring back at her were in genuine need of an explanation.

"Right, well… first things first, what a brilliant idea. Well done, Henry and the management team. What we need now is a genuine outdoors type to really sell it to us. Rob?"

Rob winced, but recovered instantly.

"Okay, for those of us who haven't a bloody clue…" He rode the ripple of laughter… "orienteering is a wonderful outdoor sport that requires a bit of brain power. Someone, possibly Henry, will have identified a number of key objectives…"

"That was me," said Scott. "I snaffled the whole thing from a friend at another company. They did it last summer and half their teams failed to finish."

There wasn't any laughter – just concern and anxiety.

"So," Rob continued, "it's basically a sport where navigational skills are used to get from point to point in varied terrain. The idea is to use the orienteering map to move speedily across country."

"Maps will be provided," said Henry.

"Yes," said Scott. "Glory awaits the first team to tick off all the points and reach the finish line. Disgrace awaits anyone who ends up lost or drowned in a peat bog."

This worried Olivia. What if the orienteering map didn't have anything helpful on it – like toilets or a café? She'd have to get googling.

"Right," said Henry. "So if you could all turn off your phones. Anyone caught cheating will be fired on the spot."

Olivia gulped.

Crap...

"Are you ready for this?" asked Laura Sneath, another likely rival in any possible job survival stakes.

"Yes, very much so," said Olivia, switching her phone off.

"Ooh, confidence," said Laura, prior to taking a bite out of an energy bar.

"I wouldn't put it that strongly," said Olivia, wondering if she could hide somewhere for a couple of hours.

Not bad thinking, Olivia...

"Hi Liv," said Deputy Assistant Director Charlotte Holberg, approaching with useless Lisa from accounts in tow. "You're with Lisa and me on this. Don't let me down."

Olivia tried not to cringe outwardly. Charlotte was the kind of boss who claimed other people's ideas as her own until things crashed and burst into flames. Then you could be assured of full credit. She also couldn't have looked more appropriately dressed in a sporty blue sweatshirt, tough jeans and sure-grip hiking boots, as if she'd known days in advance they would be orienteering – unlike Lisa, who looked less suited to the task in a chunky pink coat, beige leggings and the flimsiest white trainers.

"Commitment!" Henry declared. "It's what drives this company."

Olivia nodded. She'd seen Henry's two-year campaign to lure Zara into the stationery cupboard.

As he launched into a rallying oratory, Olivia's own thoughts on commitment surfaced. Why wasn't she dedicated to Prior Grove for reasons beyond being paid? Why couldn't she bring the passion she had for other things in life, such as…

She wondered. Did she have a passion for anything? Actual, genuine passion? There were people in this world – singers, dancers, artists, even politicians – who had a passion for the thing they did, which no doubt drove their commitment. She and Alistair had once shared a passion for doing things other people hadn't done – things that raised their adrenalin and gave them plenty to talk about at dinner parties. Well, okay, it had been Alistair's passion, but it had been enough to keep them committed to the cause.

So… passion?

She'd had plenty of passion driving her commitment to causes in the past. The young teen commitment to whip off her bra in front of Steven from next door. The late teen commitment to run the London Marathon. The twenty-something commitment to live a month in Paris to study the art scene, followed by a month in Greece immersed in the ancient world of the philosophers. It was a shame she only managed to fulfil the bra commitment, but the prerequisite of passion had burned bright in all those cases and so many more.

But now? Did she still have passion? Or was passion like a jar of pickled onions? Because, a few weeks back, she'd been sure she had a jar of pickled onions at the back of the cupboard, only to search for it and find she was mistaken.

While Henry's uninspiring speech continued with the

spirit of opportunity knocking on the door of job satisfaction, Olivia began to wonder if she might be living without passion. It seemed such a strange thing. Why hadn't it dawned on her before? And how did you go about putting passion back into your life so that you didn't end up with a soul like an empty office building at midnight?

"So, to our challenge!" Henry cried. "Scott and I will be invigilators, so no cheating. And do try to have fun. No matter how tough it gets, this is your opportunity to shine like a blazing star."

"Here are your maps and clue sheets," said Scott, handing them out. "You shouldn't find it too difficult."

"Henry's right," said Charlotte, tying her dark hair back with a pink scrunchie. "It's time to shine. We're human beings and we're built for the great outdoors. Let's get back to nature, people."

"Yeah," said Lisa, looking less likely to succeed with each passing minute.

Olivia took a map and Charlotte a clue sheet. Lisa smiled hopefully.

"Any problems, resolve them yourselves," said Henry, prior to launching into another pep talk – this one built around Game of Thrones references.

Olivia switched off at 'winter is coming' and tried to get a grip on the situation. She was about to go deep into the countryside with a member of senior management. The first objective would be to look competent.

"Let's check where we are," she said, studying the map for any sign of a folly in the middle of nowhere.

"Clue one," said Charlotte. "Take three from the pub."

Olivia narrowed her eyes and squeezed her brain.

Three... from a pub... no doubt three senior

managers who will be sitting outside in the sunshine enjoying a coffee.

The word 'perseverance' bobbed up from the morass of Henry's ongoing talk. Olivia was annoyed. If he was going to bang on all day, they could have spent more time back at the hotel, where there were facilities. Now she could only hope such a thing had been factored in to the task.

"Okay, so mini-contests," said Henry. "One team's time against another. All the losing teams will have a less pleasant weekend, I can assure you. Carla, Gianni and Joe, you'll be up against Charlotte, Lisa and Olivia. Rob, Harry and Ivana, you'll go up against Benjie, Sanjiv and Chloe…"

Olivia was appalled. They had no chance against any team that contained Carla – as in 26-year-old marathon-running, charity fundraising Can-Do Carla, who was yet another of her likely competitors in the keeping-your-job stakes. Olivia felt that just surviving the course would be a miracle. She could see it now – she and Lisa half-dead up a hillside while Charlotte sped away on an abandoned rustic bicycle to get help.

Although… wouldn't it be possible to simply follow Carla's team all the way to the finish line and then try to get past them at the death?

"Okay, so second teams, don't try to follow first teams all the way round," said Henry. "First and second teams do things in a different order and have one clue that's not the same."

Great.

"Okay, so first team ready?" said Henry. "That's Carla, Gianni and Joe. Time starts now. Charlotte, Lisa, Olivia. This is your two-minute call."

While Carla's team set off, Olivia wondered how best

to deal with Charlotte, who was busy talking with fellow senior manager Scott.

"Liv? Do you think we can win?" Lisa asked.

Olivia sometimes wondered what planet Lisa was from.

"Win? Are you serious?"

"We have to be positive, don't we? Succeeding is all about not giving up."

"Yes, Lisa, I'm sorry. I didn't mean to be negative. I just don't think we can hope for much more that finishing last."

"That's not very positive."

"Okay, tenth then."

She could almost see Lisa's brain doing the calculations.

"Sorry, Lisa. Tenth is last and I'd rather not be here."

"If I'm being honest – me neither. I could be having a coffee morning with friends."

"Exactly," said Olivia, even though, for her, it wasn't true. For so long, Saturday mornings had been a strange half-world of Alistair recovering from Friday night while trying to plan something worthwhile to do during the rest of their brief time off work. It usually meant sitting around drinking coffee while he groaned. Then, sometime between lunch and afternoon tea, he would have recovered enough to want to lure her to the bedroom. Saturday mornings nowadays were more about not having to go to work, which usually entailed being alone and watching cookery shows until lunchtime.

Henry waved his arms. "Charlotte, Olivia and Lisa, off you go. Rob, Harry and Ivana, this is your two-minute call."

Olivia's team headed up the trail.

"Look out for any helpful signs," said Lisa.

Olivia shrugged it off. There would be no helpful signs. That was clearly the point.

3

Go West! Or Possibly North...

"We're looking for a pub," said Charlotte, twenty strides into the task. "Where would you find a pub out here?"

"Um…" mused Lisa, looking left then right.

Olivia didn't mind where they found it, as long as they could join the three people already there enjoying an Americano.

"Let's make sure we win," said Lisa.

"I'll second that," said Charlotte.

"Me too," said Olivia as they progressed with what she hoped was a confident gait. She wanted Henry and Scott to admire a team that at least looked like it knew what it was doing.

A few minutes later, the path turned left and downward. It looked like a long trail to a copse of bushy evergreen trees. They pressed on. This was definitely going to be a long day.

At the trees, the path went lower and became muddy. Then, at a point where it became impassable, Lisa trod in something yucky.

"Keep to the left," said Charlotte, which meant they had to almost climb into a hedge to skirt around the goo.

Beyond the mud, the path swung upward again and then continued for about a quarter of a mile.

"Can we take a breather?" said Lisa.

"Don't be silly," said Charlotte. "We've only just started."

Olivia felt like taking a break too, but kept it to herself.

They kept on for a while, but nothing made sense on the map or in reality.

"I think we've come the wrong way," said Charlotte, handing Olivia the clue sheet.

Uh-oh. Blame time.

Olivia duly consulted it, checked the sky – in particular, the sun – and then looked back at the map. She was none the wiser.

"Which way is north?" she asked.

Charlotte looked uncertain.

"The sun rises in the east," said Lisa, "and it pointed directly in my window this morning as it rose over the folly across the valley. That means east was just off to our right before we turned left down here... which means north would be that-a-way?"

Olivia had no confidence in Lisa's accuracy but turned the north-pointing arrow on the map toward the way Lisa's finger was indicating.

"Which means we need to turn right," said Olivia. "It should lead us to a pond."

"Brilliant," said Charlotte, taking the clue sheet and the map. "We really seem to know what we're doing."

Ten minutes later, they had failed to find the pond.

"Well," said Olivia. "Either there's something wrong with the map or someone's moved the pond."

"That's not helpful," said Charlotte, handing Olivia the

map and clue sheet.

This was the beginning of the end. A bad day would mean a bad outcome on the job-saving front. Olivia knew all too well that she hadn't shown enough eagerness at work. She always did a good job, but she lacked the passion for it. That had probably become evident.

She needed to show a renewed enthusiasm for what the company did – the dark side of public relations. Not championing the popularity of celebrities but influencing all levels of government to look kindly upon the projects of Prior Grove's corporate clients. After all, you didn't give up on ten years at a firm without a fight – and the severance payment of around eight grand would be gone in no time.

"It could be we've confused north with west," she said. "Then it would be back over there."

Charlotte's hand hovered, uncertain as to whether to reclaim the map and clue sheet.

Five minutes later, they were in a field. Olivia felt disheartened.

"No sign of a pub," said Lisa unhelpfully.

"Okay, a quick three-way split," said Charlotte. "Olivia, a hundred yards that way, Lisa, the same that way. I'll try up here. We're looking for a pond or a pub."

Olivia trudged over a brow. There was no pub or pond, just lots of squat trees and rotten, brown apples littering the ground. She tried a hundred yards the other way, to another brow. In the distance was a golf course. It wasn't on the map, so she deduced that Henry and Scott must have photo-shopped it out.

"Anything?" Charlotte asked as Olivia came back.

"Just golfers."

"God, I'm bursting," said the returning Lisa. "Are we sure there aren't any public toilets on the map?"

"There's a golf course over that way," said Olivia. "There should be facilities in the club house."

Charlotte laughed.

"Take three from the pub. The nineteenth hole?"

"Brilliant," said Lisa. She turned to Olivia. "Golf has eighteen holes," she explained. "The pub is always called the nineteenth hole."

"I know that, Lisa."

"Take three away," said Charlotte. "We want the sixteenth."

They hurried to the club house, which had a lovely bar serving coffee and alcohol. It was called 'The 19th Hole'.

Cajoled by Charlotte, they used the facilities quickly and then hurried off to make progress *sans* coffee.

Behind reeds between the 16th green and 17th tee lurked a small pond. Just beyond it, a wooden bridge crossed a meandering stream.

"Right, next clue," said Charlotte. "Go. Stop. Up. Left. Name."

They headed off along the path, which soon took them away from the golf course and along another muddy lane.

The lane got worse. And worse.

"Arghh," said Lisa. "I've trodden in something nasty."

"Not more cow dung?" said Olivia.

"No, it's a dead…" Lisa lifted her foot. "…thingie."

It appeared that Lisa had trodden in a dead bird, possibly a crow, and was now wearing it like a feathery slipper. Except this slipper was maggoty.

"Kick it off," said Charlotte.

Lisa flicked her foot and the dead bird took flight… straight into Olivia's face.

"Arghh!" Olivia fell onto her backside with a squelchy thump. The wet seeped in fast. If she hadn't been sure before, she was dead certain now – this was the wrong sort of countryside.

"Oh well," said Lisa. "At least it was a soft landing."

They pushed on, now feeling like wartime commandoes rather than office workers.

"Come on, keep up!" called Charlotte from twenty yards ahead.

"Be honest," said Lisa, "we'd both rather be at home."

"You could be right," said Olivia.

Home...

Possibly with Gerry, although he so rarely stayed over these days. Up until two years ago, it would have been with Alistair, her husband of twenty years until he left. He would have had palpitations at the thought of her losing her job. He liked to do things, go places and see people, which, on top of their mortgage, cost a lot of money. In the early years of their relationship, when they talked about starting a family – well, okay, when Olivia talked about starting a family...

It hardly mattered now, but, for Olivia, the sudden termination of her life with Alistair had felt like a death in the family. Not that she grieved. You can't grieve when nobody has died. Besides, within days, a guest on The One Show said that hope and joy can be found in the most unlikely places if the heart is open. So, instead of wallowing in self-pity, Olivia opened her heart and got Gerry. Okay, so he was a married man, but he was on the verge of divorcing his wife – hence Olivia had at least found hope *of* joy.

"Let's try another split," said Charlotte. "I'll try up there. You two try the other side of that gate thing then split left and right."

Olivia hated Charlotte. The 'gate thing' had a muddy puddle either side.

"Come on," she said to Lisa.

Reaching the gate thing, Olivia tiptoed into the water and tried the metal clasp.

"The stupid thing won't open."

"Looks like someone's screwed it shut," observed Lisa. "Have you got a screwdriver?"

Olivia baulked. "Of course I haven't got a bloody screwdriver."

"We'll have to climb it then."

"Climb it? You might as well ask me to climb Mount Everest."

"I'll go first."

"No, Lisa, I'll go first. I cannot believe we have to do this crap to keep our jobs."

Olivia grabbed the frame of the gate thing and placed a foot on the first bar.

"Have you ever climbed one of those before?" asked Lisa.

"No, but I had a six-foot-six boyfriend once, so it's not much different."

Olivia reached the top and attempted to swing her leg over. It got halfway and kind of hovered.

"Lisa? Could you...?"

Lisa waded into the two inches of water and took hold of Olivia's foot. She pushed it up onto the top of the post.

"Okay?"

"No, I'm stuck."

"Perhaps I'll go back and get Charlotte."

"Stay there, Lisa!"

Olivia tried to get her leg over the top. She succeed but failed to get any more of her body over, so that when she began to slide and turn upside-down, the leg hooked over the top was all she had to prevent a complete headfirst plummet into mud and water at Lisa's feet.

"Lisa? Could you try to help in some way?"

Lisa took hold of Olivia's free leg and tried to lift it.

"Lisa, if my lady bits rip up to my belly button, I'll kill you!"

"I'll get help."

"No, don't leave."

All the same, Lisa set off leaving Olivia, free leg dangling, to sigh upside-down. In her decade with Prior Grove, she had been on eight team-building weekends, each of them ever more miserable in different ways – from pass the orange without using limbs to herding sheep and learning to pole vault. As far as she was concerned, management would forge a better team spirit by giving an undertaking that there would be no more team-building weekends.

"Hey!" It was Lisa hurrying back. "Rob's coming."

"Rob?"

"He'll have a dozen pics on his phone before you can pull the knickers out of your bum crack."

"What shall I do?"

"You'll have to sacrifice yourself, Olivia. Just fall into the mud. You'll soon be back on your feet."

"I am *not* doing an Olympic dive into two inches of sludge!"

Olivia's self-preservation wriggling resulted in just one outcome – her phone falling out of her pocket. It squelched onto a muddy ridge and started ringing.

Lisa rescued it and answered.

"Olivia's phone... yes... hang on."

She handed the phone to her upturned colleague.

"Oh... thanks... hello?"

"Olivia Holmes?"

"Yes?"

"Ah wonderful. I'm Jo Swann of Little, Green and Swan Solicitors."

"If this is about that tank…?"

"It's to do with the will of your Great Aunt Gloria."

"My what?"

"It's Rob!" cried Lisa.

Olivia sacrificed herself by plummeting headfirst into the mire, and then climbing to her feet, wobbling a bit, and running away with Lisa.

"Sorry, could I call you back?" she said into the phone. "I'm a bit busy right now."

4

Where There's A Will

Olivia didn't mind taking the Thursday off work. Despite it being a dull, cloudy morning, the train journey down to Kent was beginning to feel like an adventure. She had never attended the reading of a will before and had assumed that kind of thing only happened in old British mystery movies.

Of course, Alistair would have been straightforward on the matter. Did the old girl own a house? If so, ask if there's been a valuation and if any tax is outstanding.

She wondered what Gerry would say. Why hadn't she told him? When he came round last night for a meal and more, he had pressing business matters on the brain and so she found she had no desire to talk of wills and great aunts. Not that Olivia was convinced she would inherit much. Being a lowly great niece, her guess was a trinket or two.

Trinkets would be good, though, especially something small and silver. The family silver – wasn't that a thing? Olivia had no family – at least, no family she knew of, so family silver seemed a strange but alluring prospect.

Great Aunt Gloria…

Olivia could vaguely recall meeting her once around thirty-five years ago, but the woman herself was just a wisp of a memory. A thin face and a pale blue dress that made her look like a piece of summer sky floating around to cheer people up – although Olivia felt there hadn't been much cheer. It had been at a pub in the countryside – Kent, obviously – but the reason for that meeting escaped her. There had been wine though. That was one thing Olivia recalled strongly. Not tasting it, but sniffing it. As a nine or ten-year-old with an untutored nose, it seemed to smell of sweaty armpits. Olivia's mum and dad had been there, bless them. But the occasion? It was too many years ago to piece it all together. And having no family left, there was no-one she could ask.

She opened the magazine that had come with the free newspaper. The article began, "I dropped five dress sizes so my man could make love to the woman he married."

Marriage.

She glanced out of the window as the train roared through a small station – too fast for her to read any signs.

Twenty years. No children, of course. Alistair had been firm on that right from the start. She had thought he might mellow, but he never wavered. And that time she fell pregnant, just for three months, she spent much of it wondering how to tell him. Of course, it never came to that. She miscarried and wrapped the whole thing up in a 'gyno issues' approach. Jamie would have been sixteen had he or she lived.

Olivia concentrated on the countryside whizzing by under a November sky. Thankfully, there were a few breaks in the clouds where a little blue poked through.

Jamie would have loved this trip to the countryside. Olivia knew that for sure, because her precious, much-missed boy or girl – hence the neutral name – was very keen on horses.

She let her mind wander... a teenager on horseback... racing across the fields...

Go Jamie...

Okay, so what *exactly* might she inherit? She assumed she would get something moderately substantial – after all, why would a solicitor invite her down to Kent for a trinket or two... or to reveal that a long-forgotten relative had left everything to charity? Not that Olivia disapproved of charity being the beneficiary. Although, a little money would help with the burden of the large re-mortgage she had taken on in order to pay Alistair for his half of their apartment in New Cross.

A property though? Surely, if this long-lost great auntie owned anything valuable, like a gorgeous character cottage, there would be a closer relative laying claim to it.

You could dream though.

A beautiful 17th Century country cottage... something the Bronte sisters might have lived in had they been Kentish girls. Yes, Olivia loved the countryside. Well, not the pigsty and cowpat countryside. Not the hornet and rodent countryside. Not the stupid orienteering countryside or the three-mile walk to the nearest convenience store countryside. No, the other countryside. The one they used in Jane Austin screen adaptations. The one they used in TV adverts for butter. *That* countryside.

She flicked over a few pages of her magazine to a story of a London backpacker who had walked all the way around America's edges, from the Great Lakes to New York and then down to Florida and west to the Mississippi and so on. The idea was to learn about

America. The article contained a few selfies and mentioned some cities. It never said what the backpacker had learned about America though. It was the kind of formula Alistair loved. Go places – take a selfie – boast about it at dinner parties.

Olivia once annoyed him in front of his mates when one of them started showing off Barcelona selfies. Olivia asked him to reveal the best thing he'd learned about the city and its people. She never did get an answer.

Olivia left the train at Fallonbridge and remained on the platform to watch it trundle off deeper into Kent under a rapidly-improving sky. In no time at all, there was total silence. This was something she rarely got in London. It felt wonderful – like a warm bath. The only other person to have stepped off the train – a woman in her sixties – had already departed.

Such peace and quiet. Olivia breathed it all in and sighed it all out.

But she was on a mission. There were trinkets to be had. She just wished she could recall a little more about her great aunt, because it felt wrong to be coming for her necklace, brooch or whatever when the woman herself had been reduced to little more than a ghost long before she left this world.

The communiqué from the solicitor said it was just a few minutes' walk to the office, so Olivia exited the station and walked past the cab rank. Just ahead, the other woman had stopped to study some papers.

Olivia paused a moment. What if this turned out to be life-changing? What if they told her she'd inherited ten million pounds? She almost laughed.

The other woman set off again. Olivia followed. It seemed likely they might be heading for the same appointment. But would that make the silver-haired woman in a green raincoat and sensible footwear a relative?

A few minutes later, the woman crossed the street, came to a halt, dithered, and then entered a door alongside a local estate agent's premises. A moment later, Olivia beheld the brass plaque that told her she had arrived.

"Olivia?"

She looked up to see a young woman with short brown hair and red-framed glasses leaning out of an open window.

"Hello, yes?"

"I'm Jo. The door's open. Just push."

Olivia did so and was soon upstairs in a small office with Jo, the solicitor responsible for dealing with Great Aunt Gloria's estate, and the other woman.

"Do you know Sue?" Jo asked.

"Er, no," said Olivia, looking expectantly from Jo to the mystery woman.

"Hello, Olivia," said Sue. "I'm your cousin."

Olivia felt a flutter. She had no family she knew of… until now. A cousin! The same height and with the same round face shape. And similar eyes!

"Hello Sue. Lovely to meet you. I think I followed you from the station. To be honest, I didn't know if I had any family left. Well, I guessed there might be someone somewhere, but… well… this must be the first time I've seen a relative of mine in twenty years."

"We've met before," Sue said. "It was in a pub a few miles up the road from here. You must have been ten or so at the time."

"Yes, I remember the pub and Great Aunt Gloria making a speech about something. Not much else though."

The roar of a sports car pulling up outside interrupted them. Jo went to the window.

"It's your cousin Milo."

Olivia felt weird. Two cousins? In one day?

A moment later, a lean, dark-haired man in his twenties wearing smart shiny black shoes, smart black trousers and a smart white silk shirt was being greeted by Jo.

"Milo, this is Olivia and Sue, your cousins."

"Cousins?" Milo looked as surprised as Olivia. "I didn't know I had any family."

"Me neither," said Olivia. "Well, as I was saying to Sue, I guessed there had to be one or two lurking in the family tree, but…"

"I knew your parents, Milo," said Sue, which had a strange effect. As far as Olivia could tell, Milo didn't wish to dwell on it.

"I nearly didn't come," he said. "A reading of someone's will? I didn't even know she existed."

"Well, we're all here now," said Jo, who had been standing back a little. "How about we get things under way."

She showed them into an adjoining office furnished with a desk and computer, a potted yucca plant, and some law books in an antique cabinet.

"I'd offer you tea or coffee," she said, "but there isn't time at the moment – for reasons that will soon become clear."

They took their seats and waited to find out what was going on. To Olivia, it all seemed very odd.

"So," said Jo, "thank you all for coming this morning. I know it's a long way, but I think you'll be intrigued. I'll give you each a copy of all the relevant paperwork in due course, but first allow me to read the will's opening statement."

Jo let that hang there for a moment, as if she were the host of a TV quiz show trying to build the tension. Then she read aloud…

"I, Gloria Jane Walsh, being of sound mind and body, do hereby bequeath an equal interest in the property known as 'The Vines', Colshot Lane, Maybrook, Kent, to the following persons: Susan May Corbett, Olivia Jane Holmes and Milo Ivor Bridge."

"A property?" said Milo. "What, like a third each?"

Jo looked up from the document.

"There are conditions attached to the bequest," she said. "The first of which is that you should visit the property. Now, I've arranged a cab to take you. Do please take half an hour to look around if you need it, then you'll be brought back here for the reading of the remainder of Gloria's will. With hot drinks and pastries, of course."

"Seems a bit weird," said Milo.

"Gloria was absolutely clear on every detail," said Jo. "The one thing I can tell you is that the property is a vineyard."

"A vineyard?" said Olivia, very likely only just pipping Milo and Sue to saying the same.

"Yes," said Jo.

"A vineyard called the Vines?" said Milo.

"Yes, hardly the most imaginative name."

"It's an actual vineyard?" said Olivia.

"Yes."

"In Kent?" said Olivia.

"Yes, it's about five miles from here," said Jo, going to the window. "Your driver's outside, so I suggest you get going now and I'll see you back here in an hour or so."

Olivia stood up with the others, thanked Jo and turned to the door. It all seemed quite ridiculous. There had obviously been a mistake. Olivia Holmes did not go around inheriting vineyards. These lawyer types – you couldn't trust them. She'd obviously inherited a few bottles of wine. Good wine, no doubt. Perhaps wine worth a few bob. You heard about that sort of thing, wine as an investment. Chateau Extraordinaire or whatever. Perhaps she shouldn't go. She could get the train back home and email Jo to have the wine sent on.

Or… perhaps there was another meaning of the word. Vineyard could be like Space, as in the entire Universe or a useful storage area under the stairs.

Olivia turned again to Jo, who was following them out of the office.

"You did say vineyard?"

"Yes, do have a good look around. It's important you get an understanding of the place."

Yes, it all made sense. There was no mistake. Along with two others, Olivia Holmes now owned a vineyard.

Ha!

A vineyard.

Ha ha ha ha bloody ha!

It was the stuff of dreams and it was happening to Olivia Holmes. She couldn't wait to see it.

5

The Vines

During the cab journey to the vineyard, the clouds closed in again and it began to rain. Meanwhile, Olivia explained how she worked in public relations, although she omitted it being in a shady corner of the business. Sue, it transpired, was sixty-four and worked part-time in a school office near where she lived in Harrow, northwest London. She admitted to being a little concerned about retirement, especially after losing Bob, her husband of thirty-seven years. Milo, meanwhile, was Sue's opposite. At twenty-four, he was the confident professional embarking on a career as a junior lawyer at a major corporate firm in the City. He was currently renting a flat in Islington but would soon be buying. He had the effect of making Olivia want to exaggerate her own achievements.

"Last time I saw Gloria she was launching some hideous wine," Sue told Milo. "It was in a pub down this way. Olivia was there."

"Yes," said Olivia, "although I was nine or ten at the

time and can barely remember her. What was she like?"

"I hardly knew her," said Sue. "A couple of family occasions years before the wine thing – that's it, really."

"The vineyard connection," said Milo. "Shame the wine was no good."

"It was her husband Charlie's passion," said Sue. "Gloria carried it on after he died. I remember there was a toast. I can see Gloria now, raising her glass."

"What was the toast?" asked Olivia.

"To family."

"Family?" Milo scoffed. "How ironic. We're the only family and none of us ever visited her."

"Poor Gloria," said Olivia. "I feel a bit sorry for her."

"Yes, well," said Sue, "I remember us all saying how we'd meet up again. You know, go down to Gloria's next wine launch. Make it an annual affair, sort of thing. It never happened."

Up ahead, a sign welcomed careful drivers to the village of Maybrook. Olivia felt a shiver of excitement.

This is it.

She tried to frame in her mind what she hoped to gain from the day. So far it had given her two cousins, which was great, if slightly odd, as they weren't the kind of people she would necessarily have imagined being related to. But what if this sweeping countryside estate offered them a chance to become rural people? Would any of them take it?

The village looked picture postcard pretty, with its long High Street lined with a church, a variety of shops, and a couple of pubs – although no railway station. Then the road veered around a left-hand bend to reveal a petrol station and workshop on the right. A hundred yards on, they turned left into the narrow Colshot Lane.

Olivia instantly began searching for any sign of the

Vines. After all, what did a vineyard look like? She had seen them on TV and in magazines, the lush rolling acres under an azure sky... but they were usually in Italy, France or California. Would a Kentish vineyard look the same – especially in rainy late November? And what would it look like from the road? Would the main building be a house? A factory? Would there be a tractor outside? Or a huge truck collecting thousands of bottles to take to one of the major retail outlets?

They passed a couple of cottages and then the lane curved around to the right.

"It's just up here on the left," said the driver.

"Nice cottage," said Olivia, taking in the red brick façade, gravel drive and white picket fence as they slowed.

"No, just past that one," said the driver.

They pulled up outside an old property with bay windows either side of a central door. Thanks to a couple of broken glass panes, some missing roof tiles and a collapsed front fence, it looked sad and abandoned. The only plus was the jungle of weeds hiding much of the ground floor.

"What a dump," said Milo.

"Oh, I'm sure the interior's full of old world charm," said Sue.

"It'll certainly be full of something," said Milo. "Rats would be my guess."

They left the car and strode up to the front door, which failed to improve anyone's opinion of the place.

"I wonder when the outside was last painted?" said Sue.

Milo peeled a large blistered flake off a window frame. "Not in our lifetimes, Sue."

"There's a plaque up there," said Olivia, indicating a small brown oval stuck to the brickwork next to one of the upstairs windows. The faded white lettering stated: 'The Vines'

"Is it worth looking inside?" said Sue, possibly worrying about Milo's rats.

"I think we should," said Olivia. "We've come all this way."

Milo didn't look too sure. "What if there's someone living here?"

"Squatters, you mean?" said Sue, now looking even more worried.

"I'm sure there aren't any squatters," said Olivia.

"I was thinking more of an escaped murderer," said Milo, cheekily.

Olivia lost a little of her resolve but rang the bell. There was no corresponding sound inside.

"Perhaps he's removed the battery," said Milo.

Olivia gathered her wits and put the key in the lock. "Here we go…"

The door creaked open and the smell of damp and decay wafted out.

"Hello?" Olivia called inside. "Anyone there?"

"Thing is," said Milo, "if it's an escaped murderer or a rat, we might not get an answer."

"I'm sure it's fine," said Olivia, stepping inside and making a squelchy sound underfoot… prior to her foot continuing its downward trajectory through the carpet and floorboard to a hidden level twelve inches below.

"Well, I've seen enough," said Milo. "It's a complete shithole."

"We could always try to improve it," said Olivia, taking Sue's hand to extricate herself.

"How?" said Milo. "By knocking it down?"

"I'm serious," said Olivia, checking her shoe for dirt… or worse. "We could try to restore it."

"I'm sorry," said Milo, "but it would take a lot of time and money just to get it back to the level of a total dump. I mean look at it!"

He backed up along the path to get a better perspective of the whole. Sue and Olivia joined him.

"I can't imagine Great Aunt Gloria living here," said Sue. "How absolutely soul-destroying."

Olivia couldn't really disagree.

"No offence, Sue," said Milo, "but how is Gloria your great aunt? I mean there's not much age difference."

"Flippin' cheek," said Sue. "If you must know, Gloria was my gran's youngest sister. Veronica was the eldest."

"Kitty was my gran," said Olivia.

"Mine too," said Milo.

"Gloria was one of three sisters," said Sue. "Our ages all make sense if you pay attention to the family's birth dates."

"Sorry Sue," said Milo. "I wasn't suggesting you were ninety or anything."

"We all get old. I can only think of poor Gloria living alone here. What a dreadful thing."

"That's family for you," said Milo. "Nobody cares. Look at this place. Decay and rot. I suggest we don't explore it any further. It's a bloody death trap."

Olivia stepped up to the front door to pull it shut. But despite Milo's warning, she wanted to see more.

"Right," she said. "I'm going to take a peek around the back. I'm dying to see the vineyard."

She set off for the side of the house without waiting for an answer.

"I'm not raising any hopes," said Milo, grudgingly following.

All three negotiated the overgrown side path and pushed through a broken gate to reach a rear patio with weeds growing through every crack. Ahead, lay a garden where a barbecue might be enjoyed, once Nature's excesses had been tamed.

Crossing the garden led them to another fence and broken gate, through which lay a wide and lengthy expanse of barren, twisted, overgrown trunks and branches loosely clinging to long runs of wood and wire framework.

"Where's the vineyard?" said Milo.

"This is it," said Olivia.

"No," said Milo, "this is the evil forest from Lord of the Rings."

"It does seem quite uncared for," said Sue.

"Uncared for?" said Milo. "I'm waiting for the Dark Lord's elf assassins to come creeping out of it."

"Well," said Olivia, "the question is what do we do with it? The house and the vineyard, I mean."

"It's obvious," said Milo. "We sell it."

"Would we get much?" asked Sue.

Milo scoffed. "For Chateau Chernobyl? I doubt it."

"I'm sure someone would buy it," said Sue.

"You're right," said Milo. "Sorry, I was being flippant. Do we know how many acres we have?"

"No," said Olivia. "It looks like it goes on a fair way."

"The fact is agricultural land isn't worth much," said Milo. "I suppose if we got five to ten grand an acre, multiplied by what, five acres? Ten? The house probably adds two hundred thousand. We might get two-fifty all in. Around eighty grand apiece? That wouldn't be a bad day's work."

"Is there nothing to be said on the production side?" said Olivia without much belief. "I mean if we put some money in and produced wine?"

Milo looked set to laugh but stopped himself.

"No," he said. "But that's just my opinion. Personally, I reckon the amount of money you'd need to put this place on its feet would take years to recoup through wine sales. Again, that's just my opinion. Feel free to shoot me down in flames."

Olivia sighed. "Oh well."

"This isn't some idyllic dream," Milo went on. "This is a nightmare waiting to happen. Seriously, eighty grand apiece and you could book a lifetime of vineyard trips. That wouldn't be too terrible, would it?"

"No, I suppose not," said Olivia. "What you say makes a lot of sense."

Milo's phone rang.

"At least we get a signal."

He moved away for privacy.

"I'm such a fool," said Sue. "Did you see Milo's reaction when I mentioned his parents?"

"Um…?"

"Milo's mum was the only one who sent me a Christmas card and that stopped about seven years ago."

"Oh."

Olivia thought about that. A Christmas card from a relative. She couldn't recall ever receiving one.

"I have to say it's strange being with relatives," she said. "I've been the only one in my family for a while now."

"Me too," said Sue.

Olivia left a pause, suspecting that Sue was thinking of her departed husband.

"So you didn't contact Milo after the Christmas cards stopped?" she eventually asked.

"I didn't want to be a bother," said Sue. "It wasn't as if he knew me."

"Yes, well, now the family has its hooks in him again.

Luckily, it's only us. The last thing I want to do is dredge up painful memories for him. Best we stick to the here and now, Sue."

"Agreed."

"Well, I've had enough," said Milo, returning after his call. "The drive is sinking, the outbuildings are falling in, the main house is a disaster… I don't want anything to do with it."

"Are you sure it wouldn't make a good investment opportunity?" said Olivia.

"Not for me."

"Sue?"

"Well, I don't drink wine. Just the occasional gin and tonic."

"This wouldn't be about drinking it, Sue. It would be about making it."

"Yes, of course. I'm just saying it's not a particular passion of mine."

"It's not a particular passion of mine either, but… the house has character."

"Now you're making things up," said Milo.

"Imagine the stories an old house like this has to tell," said Olivia. "I bet a lot has happened here. And, if someone were to renovate it…"

"Who knows what new stories might come to life," said Sue, completing Olivia's thought.

"Selling it makes the most sense," said Milo.

Olivia nodded. The idea of getting around eighty thousand pounds certainly had an appeal.

6

Gloria

On the way back to the solicitor's office, Olivia continued to explore the idea of having relatives. It still seemed like a novelty, as if they were at a children's party and had been put together in a role-playing game. But a question had begun to emerge – one she suspected wouldn't go away for a while. Could she, Sue and Milo become some kind of family to each other for real? And if so, could Sue liven up a little and Milo stop faking being cool?

And what of Gloria? One minute she didn't exist in Olivia's world, and now she was making big waves.

Back in Jo's office, there was much discussion about the Vines and its state of disrepair. Jo eased all immediate concerns with coffee and pastries and the cousins were soon settling into their seats to learn more of Great Aunt Gloria's bequest.

"As you know," said Jo, "Gloria passed away in September. What you probably don't know is that she made a short video in order to address you personally."

There was much muttering. Olivia now really did feel

this was turning into an old British movie.

"Before we watch the film," said Jo, "I need to point out that everything Gloria says in the video is written into the will, so it's all quite legal and binding. I would ask you to prepare yourself for her straightforward tone. She wasn't one for polite chit-chat. So…"

Jo pressed a button on her keyboard and all eyes turned to the screen facing them on the desk.

The first thing to come up was a legal piece stating how the following film related to the last will and testament of Gloria Jane Walsh and should be seen solely as a personal presentation of the will's key points.

Then a thin, elderly, white-haired woman appeared. She was dressed in black and was seated beside Jo's antique cabinet.

"Hello, I'm Gloria Jane Walsh," she said in a measured but slightly musical tone. Her blue eyes were piercing and stared unflinchingly at the camera, at the viewer. "I've personalized my last will and testament on video because I wanted to talk to you directly. It's important to me that you understand my intentions without the need to interpret my words. I don't want you reading the will and thinking she said x but she probably meant y. I want you to be absolutely clear about the opportunity I'm affording you. Initially, I wasn't sure what to do with my estate, but my doctor tells me I don't have long, so the timing couldn't be better."

Olivia cringed a little, while, on the screen, Gloria consulted her notes before continuing.

"Condition One: At least one of you must accept all the conditions of the bequest or the property will be sold at auction and all proceeds awarded to Nick Poultney…"

Olivia tensed up. "Sold?"

"Nick who?" asked Milo.

"All will become clear," Jo reassured them.

Gloria continued. "Should at least one of you accept, all three will be considered to have met the conditions of the will."

Gloria glanced at them from the screen before checking her notes again.

"Condition Two. Having met the first condition, I want my old home to be lived in for what I'm calling the grape-to-glass cycle. That means a period beginning with pruning, through fresh buds, flowering, grape growth, harvest, fermentation and, finally, handing a bottle of sparkling wine to my legal advisor, Jo Swann of Little, Green and Swan Solicitors. That's a minimum of one year should you wish to produce a wine like cat's pee. Longer, if you go for a quality fizz. I'm allowing you the choice."

"A year?" Milo questioned.

Olivia was mesmerized to the point she feared losing touch with reality.

Gloria continued. "This means at least one of you must live at the Vines. It can be one of you full-time, or any combination of the three of you taking turns. That's up to you, but there will be at least one of you living there and sleeping there for at least a year."

Olivia swallowed drily.

"We could cheat," said Milo in a loud whisper. "Just leave a stuffed scarecrow in the bed then buy a bottle of plonk from Tesco."

"An adjudicator will keep an eye on you," said Gloria, "so there will be no cheating. If you are caught cheating, the property will be sold and you will get nothing."

Milo sighed and Gloria continued.

"Condition Three. I expect you to produce a fair harvest from my seven acres. I've worked out what tonnage is reasonable for all kinds of weather and disease patterns. While I paid for help during the season, you will not be permitted any physical or manual assistance until harvest time. Then you should get as many people as possible to help you. My adjudicator will affirm whether you've made the effort or not. Simply cultivating a few vines to get enough grapes to make a few bottles means failure. Failure means you lose your inheritance to Nick Poultney. You have a quota to reach, so get off your backsides and reach it."

Any warmth Olivia had felt toward her dead relative, any sympathy or sorrow, was now dissipating.

"She's nuts," said Milo.

"*Was* nuts," corrected Sue.

Olivia concurred.

"You may find my terms unusual," said Gloria, "but you need to understand how much I came to struggle at the Vines. It was my dear, dear husband's passion, not mine. The only aspect of it I could see that might have been worthwhile was its power to draw the family together with regular visits and growing bonds. I have to say I will reach the end of my life deeply disappointed at the response. Charlie had a passion for the wine-growing business and I have respected that. This is why my first thought was to auction the place and send the money to Nick. He's a very successful, very distant relative. Distant as in he's a third cousin twice removed or some-such and also distant in that he runs a large wine-making business in New Zealand. The thought of the extra funds boosting his multi-million dollar wine empire would meet with my Charlie's approval, while the thought of me handing it over to family members who would sell it on Day One would have him spinning in his grave."

Jo paused the video.

"There's more," she said, "but I just want to remind

you that all this is in the will in legal terms. I've checked out Nick Poultney and he is indeed a successful wine-maker in New Zealand. So successful, in fact, that he would hardly notice Gloria's estate being handed over to him."

Jo resumed the video. Gloria looked determined.

"This is my offering to you and to the memory of my dear Charlie. My only motivation is that you do not get to spend money on yourselves without respecting what has gone before. I have spies who will check on you. Any cheating and the Vines will be sold immediately leaving you with nothing. Think carefully about that. I'm reliably informed the auction value in its current state would be around two to three hundred thousand pounds. However, an architect friend tells me a complete, high quality restoration of the main house, outbuildings, vinicultural facilities and extensive replanting and maintenance would raise the value of the Vines significantly. I'm not bothered if you fail. If I'm honest, I just want you to know how it was for me, living there. I don't mind if you walk away today and reject this opportunity. Anyone not willing to make a commitment of a year to a vineyard shouldn't be allowed near one. But if you have some spirit, why not give it a try? Think about it. Good luck and goodbye."

Jo clicked the video off.

"My first duty is to ensure you fully understand Gloria's intentions."

"I assume this isn't contestable," said Sue.

"Everything's contestable," said Milo. "It's whether it's winnable."

"Whether you contest the conditions of the will is a matter for you," said Jo. "Personally, I'd say it's water-tight and you would be wasting your money. Either way, until a court of law annuls Gloria's instructions, you must comply with the conditions or lose your inheritance."

"Did she leave any cash?" asked Milo.

"Not relating specifically to the three of you, no. The money she left will help with wine production costs from this year and next, but I'll make those payments on her behalf. Most of her money went to a number of charities. There was also a little inheritance tax to pay off. Now, if I can turn to the grape-to-glass element, you'll need to know that pruning must take place before the vines begin to grow again. With just the three of you, I'd begin in early December otherwise you'll be off to the worst possible start. Either way, at least one of you must be living there from the first Monday in December. That's assuming you wish to take up the challenge?"

"That's less than two weeks away," said Sue.

Olivia found an urge rising.

"I want to try," she said. "Owning a vineyard for a year could be fun."

"That's great," said Milo. "Job done."

"Hold on," Olivia baulked, "I don't mean I want to live there for twelve months on my own. I'm thinking we should take turns."

"Sorry, I thought you were volunteering to move in. Yes, okay, well I'm really busy at work right now… and beyond Christmas too. I could probably do a few weeks in June or July?"

"I'd rather not do January or February," said Sue. "My joints play up in the cold and damp."

Olivia didn't like the idea of spending the whole winter there. How would she get to work? Was this the failure of their attempt before they had even tried?

"We need a bigger commitment," she said. "All three of us need to take it in turns."

"I've already offered what I can," said Milo. "How am

I supposed to get the time off work? Sue, you're nearly retired…"

"I can't give up my job, Milo," Sue insisted. "Couldn't you take a gap year?"

"I'm not a bloody student, Sue."

"Great," said Olivia. "We've only been a family an hour and we're already having an argument."

"Well, let's be honest," said Milo. "If I take a year off work, I'll lose fifty grand in salary. What would Sue lose? Twenty?"

"I don't see what that has to do with anything," Sue protested.

"You could live there for a year then we could sell it."

"Someone's going to have to work damned hard to produce a crop, young man," Sue said sternly. "I'm sixty-four, not twenty-four like you."

"Okay," said Jo. "I can see you have much to discuss."

"Yes, we do," said Olivia. "Very much so. And I think we should take a few days to consider the situation before we jump to any conclusions."

"Agreed," said Sue.

"Yes, fine," said Milo.

Olivia smiled at Jo, grateful that their arguing had ended for now. The question was – what would happen once they had finished their deliberations?

7

Shaz... Gerry...

The following morning, as the jam-packed District Line train lurched to a halt at St James's Park Underground Station in Central London, a boot crushed Olivia's foot. Then the doors opened to expel her onto the platform and up the stairs to street level. She barely noticed the mass movement of people – her thoughts were focused on another day at the office and the whispers continually circulating that only those showing real commitment could hope to avoid the chop. So how would she motivate herself to overcome the usual lack of drive? Was it simply a visualization mantra?

I am a motivated public relations consultant.

It seemed to lack something.

Motivation, mainly.

Maybe it was just more luck she needed – like the good fortune that came her way while orienteering. Who would have thought the final clue would prove beyond everyone but Olivia? A vague Apple Store reference giving her all she needed to get them back to the unmarked orchard she'd stumbled across earlier in the task.

Exiting the station into Petty France for the short walk to Buckingham Gate, she blinked in the late-November sunlight. Maybe she could hotwire the luck thing by consulting with higher forces, the Fates, the Great Unknown…

O wondrous Great Universal Power… are you there?

"Olivia?"

It was Shaz, Senior Director of Operations and lovechild of Voldemort and Cruella de Ville.

"Morning Shaz."

"Just the person I want. IT dug up an archive of contacts we had between 1998 and 2010. I want you to go through each entry and… well, it's a kind of 'where are they now'. There might be a few people we could hook up with again."

"After a decade or two?"

"Positivity wins the day, Olivia. It's just a couple of thousand names and I need someone I can trust to be thorough. If I give it to one of the young oiks, I'll get it back within the hour. I know you'll go through it like a crime scene investigator. Do you watch those CSI shows?"

Olivia didn't, but pretended she did, which made the side-by-side walk to the home of Prior Grove all the more uncomfortable.

Entering the large, open-plan office, Olivia paused to take in the vista of workstations dotted around in twos and threes amid pillars, potted plants, printers and a water cooler – and the line of glass-fronted managers' offices overlooking said vista.

Rapidly feeling warmer, she peeled off her coat and placed it over a vacant chair. Being an east-facing office, the ambient temperature at the start of a sunny day was always ideal for anyone in swimwear.

Popping into the kitchenette, she filled the kettle and checked her make-up.

"Morning Olivia," said Carla, whizzing by.

"Morning Carla," Olivia called back at the swirling vortex of ambition trailing in Carla's wake.

Olivia liked Carla. Well, everyone liked Carla. Not only was she a marathon-running charity fundraiser, she also happened to be super-efficient at her job.

Olivia sighed. After careful reflection, she was now sure it was a case of Carla and Olivia, along with Rob, Laura and Zara fighting for three, possibly four jobs. Why couldn't management just say so?

Having made her tea, Olivia grabbed her coat and made for her desk, a full sixty feet away from the glass temples of power.

"Morning, Liv," called Rob from the other far corner.

"Morning," she called back.

"You look radiant," said Giles as she approached.

Her senior co-worker was thirty, good-looking-and-knew-it, and based at one of a pair of desks just before her desk in the corner by the fire exit.

"Morning Giles," she said, thinking at least he looked like an adult in a business suit, whereas Rob looked like a twelve-year-old who had borrowed his dad's outfit for a fancy dress party.

As she attempted to pass Giles, his arm shot out to halt her progress.

An index finger beckoned her closer.

"Olivia," he said softly into her ear, "you know I'd make passionate love to you right now, but Henry might take a dim view of things."

His breath on her ear lobe made Olivia shiver, but she tried not to show it. Yes, she quite liked a man talking sexy to her – just not this one.

As she settled into her chair, Laura came in looking cold. Laura always looked cold.

"God, it's like Siberia in here," she moaned for the entire office to hear.

"Stop dressing for St. Bloody Tropez then," snapped Rob. "Summer's a million miles away."

Of course, Laura rarely overdressed for the office – otherwise Henry wouldn't get a face full of bosom every time he stopped by to ask her about absolutely nothing whatsoever.

"I'll ask Henry to check on the heating," she said.

Olivia sent death rays. If the temperature went up, it wouldn't be Laura sweating a bucket load in full view of her workmates.

Zara came in, stopping to check her phone before continuing across the office to take her seat facing Giles.

"Morning all," she trilled.

"Morning Zara," said Olivia. "How did the meal go?"

"Don't ask. It was terrible. Whoever recommended that place needs a jail sentence."

It was Laura who had recommended it – mainly because she hated Zara. That would intensify now they were rivals. Olivia preferred the old days, when people left for nice reasons, like finding a new job.

She missed Cass, Zara's predecessor, who had left for a different nice reason. They had been great work buddies, going out for drinks and laughs, until Cass fell pregnant. Her twins were now approaching their third birthday, which meant Olivia only saw full-time mum Cass once every few months. It had been hard at first –

all the talk of babies. There is a particular kind of pain reserved for those who have miscarried – a pain amplified by the joy of others experiencing the simple pleasures that had been stolen away by the indifferent forces of nature. The only saving grace had been that when Cass's twins came along, Jamie would have been thirteen and so the baby discussions didn't have so much impact. More jarring around that time had been a train journey shared with two girls of Jamie's notional age, and hearing one of them say she'd rather be dead than go to a folk music festival. Rather be dead? Seriously? Olivia followed up the encounter by promptly getting herself to a local folk gig. After the show, she'd felt that Jamie would have quite liked it. It was important to know.

"Here comes trouble," muttered Giles.

It was Henry making his way down to Giles, Zara and Olivia.

"Morning troops. Any chance of having those research notes I was promised yesterday?"

"We're practically there, Henry," said Giles. "Olivia's going to check everything first."

"Hold-ups, hold-ups," muttered Henry. "A little more commitment, please. We're talking about a passionate, valued client. I expect us to be just as passionate about our support work."

"No problem, Henry," said Olivia. "It'll be with you by twelve."

Zara raised her eyes.

Bog off, Zara. Giles is NOT using me to do half his work.

"I was meant to have it yesterday, Olivia," said Henry. "It's like that film, Apollo 13. Working with very few resources, Tom Hanks amazed us with what could be achieved with a bit of effort."

"Henry, I was in Kent."

"So? Tom Hanks was in space."

Watching him return to his glass sanctuary, she thought she probably had a couple of months left. How many jobs had she applied for in the time since it became apparent there would cutbacks? Twenty applications, five interviews, no job offers. It made her realize that the years she had spent in the same role weren't seen as solid, but stale. Surely Prior Grove wouldn't get rid of her? She gave them a good day's work, day in, day out – which was more than she could say for some.

"No time for daydreaming, Olivia," said Giles in a friendly manner.

Olivia nodded and got on with her work.

The morning dragged by, but Olivia was happy enough doing Giles' job for him. At least it kept her mind off food. It never ceased to amaze her how she could be two dress sizes too big and yet always be hungry. It wasn't logical and it wasn't fair. Elevenses had proved a complete terror. People munching their way through a truckload of cookies, muffins, chocolate bars, pastries...

She held out until half-eleven and then rushed out to get a Twix, a Coke and bag of Mini-Cheddars. When she got back, Zara was waiting to pounce.

"Shaz is not happy."

"That's hardly news, Zara." As far as Olivia was concerned, Shaz was never happy.

"You do remember who Shaz is?"

"Isn't she the senior director who created all the loveliness in the world?"

"Apart from that."

"Er... the exec who dumped a crap job finding old contacts on someone? Me, in fact?"

"Shaz is not happy about something else, Liv."

Olivia sighed. "Tell me, did the Word of Shaz come down via Henry?"

"It did."

"And lo, it was revealed that Shaz isn't happy about what exactly?"

"The way the teams are set up."

"So, old news then."

"No, she's got something planned."

Olivia sighed. "We are powerless pawns in Shaz's Game of Frowns."

"I think she's serious," said Giles. "As in in serious about starting next week."

That hit home. The dreaded push-off was being speeded up. Why couldn't Shaz stay in her fifth-floor office and leave the regular staff alone? In fact, why didn't someone nail a big board over her door and trap her inside? Perhaps they could throw Henry in there too before they nailed it up.

An image of Shaz devouring Henry like a giant black widow spider popped into Olivia's head…

An email alert pinged on her desktop. It was Shaz. How many contacts had Olivia tried in two and a half hours? How many had responded? Shaz wanted to know so that she could guesstimate how much time to allow for the task.

Olivia guesstimated that Shaz wouldn't be too impressed to learn that the current total stood at zero calls and zero responses. She hadn't even been to IT to get the list.

Her potentially barren future flared up once again. What would she do about clinging on to her job at Prior Grove? And there was that other matter that had been bubbling away not far beneath the surface. What were she and her cousins going to do about the vineyard in Maybrook, Kent?

After work, she took the Tube north. Gerry had been working from home until six and so didn't want to drive all the way across London during rush hour to get to Olivia's place in New Cross.

Naturally, she knew what that meant. Over the past few months, it had become an increasingly standard alternate plan. 1) Travel up to London's northwest suburbs, at least five miles from Gerry's home, 2) Have a meal in a different restaurant each time, and 3) Drive to a hotel, motel or, too often these days, a secluded spot.

Of course, it wasn't a fault to be working hard for success – and, besides, his divorce was getting ever-nearer...

During 2, she had wanted to tell him about the Vines, but he was in a foul mood. Something was going on in the background that he wouldn't open up about. His business world was made up of four or five companies that revolved around various management advice and support services, including training and mentoring. She had lost track of which rival was stitching him up in which business. She just nodded and offered sympathy. Directly after 3 – a shabby motel – she again thought of mentioning the Vines, as he was finally in a mellower mood, but the moment passed because he had to get back home for a late-night call to Portland, Oregon.

She liked Gerry – admired him, even – and knew that he just needed to sort out a couple of things in his life. Divorcing his wife was the biggie. That marriage had failed a long time ago and Gerry was working tirelessly to bring things to a civilized conclusion. Olivia understood breakups and didn't want to make it awkward for him and his wife, Elizabeth. She just wished things could move a little faster. Maybe not as fast as Alistair the Rat's parting, but at a less glacial pace.

On the long northwest to southeast journey home, she studied a few of their photos on her phone. His boyish grin was a winner. And, despite being ten years older than her, he was still slim and active. Once they were properly together, things would improve. She held out a strong hope that love might even flourish to strengthen their commitment to each other. Until then, it would have to be nights like this, with memories not of sparkling romance, but of a speedy meal, quick physical engagement, and a long crosstown journey home to an empty apartment.

8

Morning Has Broken… And So Has The Plumbing

Olivia checked the clock. It was just after six a.m.

Ugh.

She hated waking up early on a Saturday morning. And with thoughts of the vineyard on her mind, there was no way she'd get back to sleep. That might have been mitigated had she been able to roll over into Alistair's arms, but he was elsewhere, in the arms of Stephanie, ten years his junior.

She sighed. He used to come in at half-two in the morning and make a heck of a noise with the microwave before falling asleep in front of a Hawaii-Five-O re-run. Stephanie was welcome to that. Although there had been those rare occasions when he'd wake up fresh and by now they would be hungry for each other…

It could be like that with Gerry, of course, but – just like Alistair – not often.

She sat up in bed. This was her domain now. She was

queen of all she surveyed. The comfy bed, the soft duvet, the white Ikea wardrobe, the fluffy cream carpet, and chunky white Venetian blinds...

She picked up her latest paperback and read for an hour. Then she went to the kitchen to make breakfast. Below her window, the street was still and quiet. Well, it would be at seven-fifteen.

Olivia put the kettle on. What was she going to do? She couldn't live in the tiny village of Maybrook and work sixty miles away in Central London, could she? The options for doing so weren't great. Living in Kent, she could drive to Ashford, get the high-speed train to St Pancras, and then the Tube to St James's Park – but the online journey planner said it would take two hours door to door. Driving all the way was also a two-hour trip. And with either option, there would be expensive rail tickets or expensive fuel and parking costs.

And if she did commute, what about grape production? She needed to make a proper go of it or they would lose everything to the successful guy in New Zealand.

She tried to picture it – her typical weekday at the Vines, deep in winter. Up at five, breakfast, pruning for an hour with a flashlight taped to her head, leave before seven and be at her desk by nine... and then back to Kent by half-seven with another pruning session in the dark before eating something and falling into bed.

She couldn't get her head straight. It was all very well thinking about grapes and wine, but what about her career? Could she put in the effort required to save her job and commute from Kent? Or would Prior Grove get rid of her regardless?

But... if they did, wouldn't she try to get another job in order to pay the mortgage?

She had tried. And failed.

A thought occurred. Were there public relations firms in Kent? In particular, public relations firms that would allow her seventeen weeks off this coming year?

She sighed.

It came back to the inescapable. If she wanted to make absolutely sure they inherited the Vines, she needed to quit her job and run the vineyard for a year. She could rent her apartment to someone, anyone, so their rent covered her monthly mortgage repayments. Then she'd scrape by in Kent for twelve months, sell the Vines, and have a pile of cash. Hopefully then she'd be able to get a fresh job in London. Certainly, walking away from the Vines with eighty or ninety thousand would buy her some time vis-à-vis job-hunting.

Except she didn't want to give up her job. It was a routine she liked. The idea of leaving the dark side of public relations for a whole year and then trying to get back in at the age of forty-five… well, she already felt ancient at Prior Grove. She might struggle to get a return ticket. Then the money she'd make from the Vines would dwindle unless she took up another job. But what kind of job? She hated change. She wasn't that keen to have someone live in her apartment either.

She'd agreed with Milo and Sue to possibly catch up next Wednesday to discuss their options. Away from that, she had planned to go down to Kent this very lunchtime – although now it seemed like a lot of hanging around doing nothing in New Cross until it was time to leave.

She left the kitchen. Her cup of tea would remain unmade. Instead, she showered, dressed and headed for her little red Polo.

*

Olivia smiled at the sign welcoming careful drivers to the village of Maybrook. This time she took in the fabric of the village: St Mary's Church on the left, the White Swan Chinese restaurant, a Heart Foundation charity shop, Sylvie's Flowers, Shore's the greengrocer ... then on the right, Butler's shoe and sportswear shop, the Village Bakery, Maybrook newsagents... then, on the left, the Royal Standard pub, almost facing the Old Hall pub on the right... then the Flower Power art gallery, Kelvin's the butcher, and Village Wines for beers and prosecco...

Next came a street on the right that seemed to have a lot of homes a long way down either side... then the road took a bend to the left revealing the petrol station and workshop over on the right... and a lane just past them with more homes lining it. Then it was a short distance to Colshot Lane on the left... which took her past a couple of homes before it bent round to the right.

And there it was, up on the left.

Olivia pulled up at the Vines but didn't get out of the car straightaway – she sat there and tried to take it all in. Was this living the dream? She wondered why people said that. Her last dream had involved pirates selling pickled onion wine from Belgium.

That said, this wasn't the usual dream. It involved a nutty dead relative, a pile of old bricks masquerading as a house, and a field full of overgrown vines.

She grabbed her handbag, got out of the car and stepped into semi-liquid fox excrement. Well, at least she couldn't get straight back in the car. Not unless she wanted to commit suicide by noxious gas.

She beheld the house. It was indeed a dump. There would be no quick results. Was that okay? Could she invest her time and energies in a year-long project? Of course she could. She'd make some money when they sold it. But by then she would have been a long time out of lobbying policy-makers on behalf of hidden clients. It certainly wouldn't be easy to get back in.

She cleaned her shoe on the grass before entering the house. Once inside, she wondered why she'd bothered to clean the shoe. The place stank.

"Hello?" she called nervously. "Anyone there?"

Silence.

She stepped over the hole in the floor and went into the lounge – which, compared with the entrance hall, wasn't too bad. It was a knocked-through space combining two original rooms to give a long room with views to the front and rear of the house. The threadbare chair in a rear corner facing the ancient TV set – that had to be where Gloria had spent her evenings. Possibly her mornings and afternoons too. It was a barren room, though. Apart from the chair and TV, there was an old two-seater sofa, an old glass-top table with a crack, and a new-ish sideboard that looked cheap and out of place. The carpet was trodden in with grime, the ceiling was yellow and cracked, and the walls had peeling maroon paper. There were also dried purple flowers in a tacky vase on the front windowsill, framed by part-drawn mustard curtains – which might have started life as beige.

Olivia looked to the chair again and imagined Gloria sitting there. It seemed so lonely. But what of 1962, when Gloria and Charlie bought the place? All that verve, hope and passion…

She sighed. Hope and passion… and unremembered lives.

Now Charlie's passion for growing grapes was just a silly challenge for people who had never given grape-growing a thought. Why hadn't Gloria just sold the place and given the money away?

Olivia stared into the kitchen, which looked like it required a Haz-Chem sticker on the door. She could imagine Gloria at the cooker, making a modest meal, and at the sink washing up her few bits at the end of the day.

There was a calendar on the wall. It displayed August. Was that the last time Gloria thought about life and its potential? Never to turn the page to September, the month of her death.

Olivia went upstairs.

In the main bedroom, she imagined Gloria in bed. Young and rampant... old and failing... all in the same single space over a timespan that probably flashed by all too quick.

What must it have been like in 1962? They would have been married a good few years by then, but without children. Did they buy this place hoping to raise a family? Or was it to give them such busy lives that they hardly noticed they were without offspring? Again, she tried to get a sense of Charlie and Gloria and their love, their passion, so alive in 1962, so vibrant and vital... but she sensed nothing. All she could feel was the loneliness of an old woman.

Or was that the point? After all, Gloria could have given the Vines away and Olivia would have been none the wiser. This way, Gloria lived on in three people. Okay, so she was yet to be cherished in their hearts, but Olivia, Sue and even Milo would have Gloria Walsh very much in mind, possibly for the rest of their lives.

"Gloria?" Olivia's voice sounded out of place in the bedroom. "It's me, Olivia."

Olivia waited for any kind of response. There was none, of course. If anything, the silence seemed to close in on her.

"Gloria? I'm sorry you lived here alone for so long. I

know you didn't think much of us, but I never really knew anything about you. All I'm asking is you give us a chance before judging us as useless twits from the city. For what it's worth, London can be lonely too. There are plenty of people going around without any real friends. It happens all the time. Also, until I met Sue and Milo, I wasn't sure if I had any family. So thank you for that. Thank you for giving me two cousins."

She looked around the room again.

"Where are your photos, Gloria? We've got all the paperwork, but where are you and Charlie?"

She waited a moment. Then she went to the bathroom.

"Gloria? Does your loo work?"

The bathroom was in a bad way. She knew the tank and pipes that had leaked in the loft were directly above the bathroom because half the ceiling had fallen down and she could see them.

To pee or not to pee?

The toilet bowl was empty and, by lifting the cistern lid, she could see that it was empty too – and would remain so until she could turn the water back on.

But, should you do that if there had been a leak?

It was an academic question, because she had no idea where the stopcock might be.

Stop thinking about water, Olivia.

She wondered if it would be okay to use the loo anyway? But that would be horrible for anyone popping in there after her.

She tried to forget her need and instead went outside to check on the garden and vineyard beyond.

The garden was still the same mess she had seen on her first visit, although the first breath of winter was keeping things dormant. It was clear though – at the first sign of spring, this lot would erupt into a rainforest.

Moving beyond the garden, she stared out over the twisted frames of the vines. They seemed to go on forever, although, now she looked a little closer, it seemed the nearer vines were better behaved than those triffids inhabiting the farther reaches.

She pulled her phone from her bag and thought how to best text Cass. But no, this would take an hour of texts to put her friend in the picture. With one bar of signal, it was worth attempting a call.

"Cass? It's Olivia. How are you and the family?"

"Hi Liv. We're all good. How about you?"

It was great to hear Cass's voice – all warm and friendly.

"I'm fine, but um… well… you'll never believe it, but I've inherited a vineyard."

The line went silent and Olivia checked to see if the bar had gone and she'd lost the signal.

"Cass?"

"Sorry, Liv, that was the least decipherable sentence I've heard in years. Can you repeat it?"

"I know, it's ridiculous. It's true though. I had an old great aunt who died and she's left her vineyard estate to me and my two cousins. Well, sort of."

"Hang on, this is getting less understandable by the second. You don't have any cousins."

"I know, but I do. I suppose I always wondered if there might be family out there somewhere – and now I have Sue, who's sixty-four and Milo, who's twenty-four. Good eh?"

"Yes, fab – but returning to the first piece of info?"

"Yes, well, Great Aunt Gloria owned a vineyard."

"What, seriously? A vineyard? As in France, straw hat, sitting in the sunshine, drinking fabulous wine? Or, wait, it's not Italy or Cali-flippin'-fornia?"

"No, Kent."

"Kent? As in nearby Kent. Rainy England Kent?"

"Yes, a place called Maybrook. I'll send you some photos. Stand by."

Olivia took some shots of the vineyard, the garden, the back of the house, a couple of interiors, and a selfie in the front garden with the house as a backdrop. Once she had sent them, Cass was quickly back on the line.

"Have you thought of selling it?" she said.

"We can't," said Olivia looking around the unkempt front garden. She went on to explain the ins and outs of having to inhabit the old place until they produced a sparkling wine – so at least twelve months.

"That's the craziest thing I've ever heard," said Cass. "You're not going to stay there, are you?"

"I might."

"Wow, that's a new era dawning right there. What about your place in New Cross?"

"I don't know. To be honest, we really haven't sorted out any kind of plan. We will though."

"I'll have to come and have a look then – at some point… when you've tidied it up a bit."

"Sure."

An old man was coming down the lane from the main road. Although he was on the other side, he was looking directly at Olivia.

"Let's have a proper catch-up soon, Cass."

"You bet. I'm dying to know what you decide."

"Okay, we'll synch diaries once I know what's happening. Bye."

Olivia could now see the old man had a tiny dog on a long leash. They both looked about ninety, although the old guy had an upright gait and some black strands in his silver hair. Her London instinct was to let them pass by without a word. But she was new to the countryside and wanted to put away her city ways of never saying hello to strangers. So, in the spirit of the countryside code of friendliness, she called out hello – and the old man ignored her.

Flippin' cheek.

Olivia went back inside and tried to locate the stop cock. She needed to turn the water on to get the toilet to flush. If a leaky pipe started squirting water, she could turn the supply off again once the cistern had a full tank. Only there was no sign of the stopcock under the stairs, under the kitchen sink, or anywhere else she tried.

Perhaps it was in the lane outside the front gate.

It wasn't. But in looking, she saw the old man and his dog coming back her way. Well, he could stick a good morning where the sun doesn't shine.

"Good morning," he called, crossing the tarmac to her side. "I'm Ken from just down the lane. Pleased to meet you."

Hmmm. Clearly this countryside code is going to take a bit of work.

"Hello Ken. I'm Olivia."

"I didn't stop earlier," he said. "I needed to pay a little visit, if you know what I mean."

I know the feeling.

"No problem, Ken."

He smiled, and she saw a glint in his eye – the kind that made you check you still had your wallet.

"Going to make fizz, are you?" he asked.

"Fizz?"

"It's all the rage, I hear. Charlie used to grow all kinds of grapes for flat wine, but I hear sparkling wine is what people want these days. Did you say you were going to make fizz?"

"To be honest, we haven't thought that far ahead."

"Oh, you must always think ahead with wine. Not that I know a lot about it. Just to say the vines you've got have produced good grapes over the years, but you haven't always had good wine. Luck of the draw, I expect."

Olivia reached down to stroke the dog. He seemed friendly enough.

"That's Beano," said Ken. "He's a sort of Jack Russell, probably. Anyway, my advice would be to think ahead. Charlie used to give me a couple of free cases, but it wasn't always the best. Fizz would be a much better bet."

Did he just lick his lips?

"Do you know what kind of fizz, Ken?"

"Oh, I don't know much about winemaking. Can never remember the names of the grapes. Chardonnay, pinot noir and pinot Meunier, I think. Like they use for making champagne. You can't call it champagne, mind."

"Do we have those grapes?"

"It's like I said, I don't know much about it. Whatever they planted... well, you might need to replace some of the vines. Disease and so on. I think your older vines might be Reichensteiner, Müller-Thurgau, Schönburger, Huxelrebe, Ortega and Dornfelder. I can't be sure but most of the newer vines could be what you need for sparkling wine. Anyway, nice to meet you. Good luck."

"Actually, before you go – I'm trying to locate the stopcock so I can turn the water on. I don't suppose you know where it is?"

"No idea, sorry."

"Well, where's yours?"

"Oh, mine won't turn your water on, Olivia. It's completely separate."

Good grief. "No, I meant perhaps whoever built these

houses put the stopcock in the same place."

"No, these properties all date back to different builders, different times. Some of them years apart. My stopcock's under the floor inside the front door. Yours could be anywhere."

Olivia bade him farewell and went to look for the stopcock. Sticking her head into the hole by the front door, she spied a lead pipe, which led to a tap.

Bingo.

She put her bag on the bottom stair and got down to lean into the hole. The tap was... just... about... within reach.

She turned it.

Huh?

There was a sound of water... lots of water... coming down the stairs...

"My bag!"

She tried to pull herself free of the hole, but only fell further in. Then she half-twisted, yanked herself out, lurched across to grab her handbag, slipped, put a green slimy patch on her elbow, and finally retrieved her bag, which now contained half a pint of water.

"Dammit."

She turned the water off and considered the situation. This needed a plumber, but who would pay for it? And more urgently, what would she do about her need to empty her bladder. She looked into her bag, with her things sloshing around like wreckage on a tide. That didn't help at all.

She ran up to the bathroom and removed the lid of the cistern. It had barely an inch of water in the bottom.

"Great, a million gallons down the stairs, two spits where it counts most."

She went downstairs, emptied her bag onto the

kitchen table, and ventured outside. Over to the left of the nearest vines, there was a shallow ditch.

"Oh well…"

A moment later, squatting down, she was thinking how at work she used a fully-tiled room with fragrant soap, hot water and hand dryers. Here she was using a small trench dug by animals.

Progress?

Alarm gripped her entire being. She was drowning a worm.

"Argh, no…"

She flicked the struggling, innocent creature out of the slurry and wiped her gooey finger on some straggly grass.

This is bloody ridiculous.

Extricating herself from the ditch, she looked around to make sure no one had seen her in action. Relieved – literally – she wondered how much it would cost to make the Vines habitable for the next twelve months. And how much it would cost to fully renovate once they had met the conditions of the will.

"I hope you weren't watching," she said to Gloria as she went back inside.

In the lounge, she sat in Gloria's chair and googled ways to make sparkling wine. It wasn't straightforward. First you had to ferment the wine in barrels. Then it required a secondary fermentation in the bottle to create those all-important bubbles. She tried to imagine them making an English sparkling wine to rival champagne within a couple of weeks of picking the grapes. It seemed unlikely. They would have to produce the cat's pee Gloria mentioned.

She went to the window and stared out over their acres of gnarled, overgrown vines. She needed to forget the wine. It was a case of starting at the start. But where did you actually begin? Or did you not begin and instead go back to public relations, which you knew and understood? She decided it was probably best not to make any decisions beyond heading back to London before she needed to use the ditch again.

9

Rivals

Just after nine on the Monday morning, Olivia was at Prior Grove making tea in the kitchenette while wondering how things would shape up vis-à-vis the company restructuring. Was it a case of her becoming more pro-active by going after Henry and Shaz in a campaign of usefulness, passion and commitment? After all, she was up against Rob, Carla, Zara and Laura – with at least one of them getting the boot.

"Morning," said Rob, coming in to make tea.

"Morning, Rob."

"Funny us being rivals," he said.

"Yes, hilarious."

Rob checked his phone.

"Olivia, could you do me a massive kindness and bring my tea over? Code Red emergency email to deal with."

Before she could tell him to go boil his head, he was gone.

A moment later, carrying two cups of tea, she dropped one off at her desk and then trekked across to the other corner. Halfway there, Rob called out.

"Henry? Could I get your opinion on something?"

Henry?

Olivia didn't understand… until Henry emerged from the store room by Rob's desk to witness Rob being served tea by an idiot.

"Ah, thank you, Olivia," said Rob. "So, Henry, about the best books to buy on management?"

Olivia had a sinking feeling. A real one. She was shrinking. No, hang on… Rob's desk was higher. He'd raised it on little blocks – which meant he could have his chair higher too.

While Henry launched into one of his pet subjects, Olivia skulked away hoping her stupidity wouldn't count against her.

Back at her desk, sipping hot tea, she wondered how to proceed. Wasn't her place at Prior Grove worth fighting for? After all, the Vines was beginning to show signs of becoming the headache Milo had predicted. Emails to her cousins had merely secured a vague agreement that they should do something. With their obligatory twelve-month tenure due to begin after the weekend, one of them needed to be there on Monday. But who?

Maybe the 'grape to glass' challenge was a curse. Without a unified and dedicated approach, they had no chance.

But what if she stayed there?

She imagined Christmas Day at the Vines, alone and freezing. Was this all Gloria really wanted? To make them suffer? Maybe keeping her job at Prior Grove or getting a similar job elsewhere was the real way forward. That said, it seemed crazy to forfeit the Vines on the first day.

It also seemed crazy that she still hadn't told anyone at

work about it. Why was that? What deep-seated fixation was it masking? In an ideal world, there would be no prospective job cuts at Prior Grove and she would be able to carry on enjoying a straightforward, stress-free life, dedicating herself to clients who were passionate about creating the best conditions for their empires to flourish. She would carry on taking their concerns and making it her business to influence the decision-makers and policy-shapers at any level of government, local or national. Then she would head into her fifties and sixties, and retirement, in a sensible way.

But if she left the dark side of public relations for a whole year...

Was the lure of eighty or ninety grand clouding her judgement? Was its potential to reduce her mortgage drawing her from a place of understanding to a place of otherness, a place she didn't belong, performing a range of tasks she had no aptitude for? Would the money from the sale of the Vines simply be compensation for throwing away her career? Could she let that happen? Maybe that's why she hadn't told anyone – because she didn't wish to say something that couldn't be unsaid. Of course, if Prior Grove didn't want her, that could change her thinking – although, if she wanted to remain in the public relations business outside of Prior Grove, then her best chance of joining another company would be now and not in a year's time.

Around 12.15 p.m., with the waiting time until her one o'clock lunch break seemingly stretching deep into forever – a horror compounded by early lunch-takers returning with sandwiches, wraps and God-knows-what-else – Olivia scoffed an emergency fun-size Twix. Then she took to humming a selection of Andrew Lloyd Webber show tunes in an effort to drown out Zara's eating noises.

No chance.

As far as Olivia was concerned, Zara committed three separate offences when she ate lunch *al desko*.

First there was the clicky-smacky tongue thing she had going on. It sounded like six slugs having an orgy.

Then she would finish every meal with a pot of rice or custard dessert, which she would consume inside thirty seconds – a feat that involved clunking her teeth against the metal spoon.

But that wasn't even close to being the worst part. Once the dessert had been gobbled up, she would devote at least ten minutes to noisily scraping out any remaining sub-atomic particles from the pot.

There were days when Olivia dreamed of tying Zara to a giant spoon and drowning her in a large vat of custard.

Zara also drove Giles mad, although he was more forthright than Olivia, saying things like, "That's not one of the recalled pots, is it? There was a sign up in the supermarket. Fecal matter present. Potentially fatal." Once, when Zara left a just-started banana rice dessert to grab something from the printer, Giles, in league with Rob, drew an ejaculating willy on a scrap of card and submerged it in the pot. When Zara scooped it out, Rob had to be led away with a suspected ruptured spleen from suppressed laughter.

Eventually, it was Olivia's turn for lunch. As usual, she was out of the building in a flash and across the street to the deli. While waiting to order, she got stuck between two young women discussing a third party who was quitting her job to spend a year travelling around southeast Asia. They admired her spirit, and so did Olivia. Was it really that simple? You just quit your job to spend a year in Southeast Asia, or in Olivia's case, southeast England? She felt the adrenalin surge… and her fears rising up like an army of skeletons climbing out of a tomb in a horror movie.

No, she had to stay in public relations. This was her turf. She had to fight to stay at Prior Grove. And if they got rid of her, she had to fight to get into the dark side of another public relations firm before her links to the industry grew cold and stiff. The other option – that of quitting public relations to produce a quality sparkling wine – well, that was just crazy.

Ten minutes later, she was back at her desk. This fitted in with Bountiful Overlord Shaz's view that staff using their lunchbreak as an actual break weren't really dedicated to Prior Grove. When Olivia first came to work there all those years ago, lunchtime meant walks, including the two hundred yards from the office to Buckingham Palace, where she would imagine the goings-on inside. Not anymore.

Munching on a sandwich, Olivia started looking for jobs on her phone. She didn't get far though.

"Can I have everyone's attention?"

Henry had emerged from his office, hands aloft, messiah-like, prompting Olivia to fear another dollop of tosh from '101 Ways To Motivate Employees'. She was right. Once again, Henry was banging on about commitment.

"Sum up Henry in one word?" Zara muttered to Olivia.

"Irritating."

A while later, with Henry back in his office and Zara in the Ladies, Giles came over to whisper in Olivia's ear.

Not more creepy talk…

"Zara and Rob are seeing each other. They got it going on the teambuilding weekend."

Olivia sighed. *Great.* So Zara was now working in league with Rob and had set her up. Rob certainly wouldn't think twice about relaying details of the "irritating" comment to Henry or Shaz in a jokey but effective way.

Her phone pinged. It was text from Sue.

> 'Let's forget the possible Thursday meeting. Let's meet at The Vines on Saturday. Let's say one p.m. One of us will have to be there on Monday. Let's not lose it without giving it a chance.'

Olivia was in agreement. Sue was right about meeting to discuss their options in situ, not in some comfy London pub. In fact, she would get a builder to meet them there. They needed a quote for immediate repairs to make the place habitable, and a further quote for a complete restoration and refurbishment of the entire estate should they choose to renovate it before they sold it. Then, if they chose to abandon the project, they would do so from a position of knowledge and not ignorance.

After work, she met up with Gerry in northwest London for a meal at a Chinese restaurant and a visit to a cheap hotel. When would he be leaving his wife? She had seen enough TV dramas and read enough books to know that some men lied about having a failing marriage as a way to keep a mistress keen. Was that the real Gerry? Was he just using her? When he asked what she'd been up to, she said she'd been down to Kent. But when he sounded interested, she said it had simply been a day trip.

Commitment.

There could be no sharing news of the vineyard until he got his divorce moving faster than a bewildered snail.

10

Wine Tasting For Beginners

The pub in New Cross was busy for a Wednesday evening, but Olivia and Cass found a table in the corner. Meeting up used to be a regular thing, but Olivia wasn't ignorant of the limitations Cass was under, time and money-wise. What pleased her was how Cass could still turn from maternal to carefree with just a Christmas reindeer pullover and her shoulder-length reddish-brown hair freed from the regular ponytail.

"So, you're all meeting up on Saturday now?" said Cass, having taken a gulp of cider. She'd assured Olivia that her parents had the children staying with them overnight, meaning husband Jake would also be having a rare night out.

"We were going to meet up midweek in London, but Sue suggested Saturday in Kent and that made more sense."

"So you haven't decided anything then."

"No, but the way things are, I might end up quitting my job and committing myself to Kent or not quitting my job and pretending Kent never happened."

"What if you do go? What about the flat... sorry, *apartment?*"

Olivia smiled. New York had apartments, London had flats. But now London had apartments too, because developers found they could charge more if it sounded aspirational. Olivia and Alistair bought an apartment, which did seem to cost around ten percent more than flats in the area. Of course, Alistair had felt it worth paying the extra money – which was annoying, as he no longer paid the mortgage on it.

"Okay, so the apartment. If I go to Kent full-time, I could rent out New Cross for a year. The rent money would cover my mortgage payments. On the downside, I don't want anyone living in my flat. Sorry, apartment."

"What about work? Would you commute?"

"God, that would be a total nightmare – but yes, I suppose so, if I had to. Unless I quit Prior Grove, live in Kent and get some freelance lobbying work."

"Er, Earth calling Olivia – it would take ages to get clients."

"True. To be honest, I don't know what to do. Any ideas?"

"As you say, commuting would be hard. And wouldn't you be in Kent to do things on the vineyard? That wouldn't be so easy if you were working in London and spending half the day to-ing and fro-ing."

"Yes, then there's sleeping to fit in as well. You're right – I'd do practically nothing with the vineyard."

Olivia sighed. Commitment was a long word but, to borrow one of Henry's phrases, she needed to mount it like a horse and ride it to Successville. Or she needed to shy away from it and get back to normal. All this messing around between the two worlds was driving her mad.

"What about selling the flat?" said Cass.

"Yes, but in a year's time, when we sell the Vines, I'd have nowhere to live. Getting back into public relations would be enough of a challenge, let alone having to arrange a mortgage on another property with potentially no job."

"You're overlooking something. What if you sold your flat, moved into the Vines and stayed there."

"Stayed there?"

"Yes."

"Like forever?"

"Yes, what if you took over where this great aunt left off?"

"Me become Gloria?"

"Well, you'd be able to pay off Milo and Sue, wouldn't you?"

"You haven't seen the size of my re-mortgage. I had to pay off Alistair, remember?"

"Right, so could you pay off one of them?"

"Possibly… but I'd have nothing left to do any work on the Vines, which desperately needs big bucks spent on it starting yesterday. And, at the bottom of all that, is the fact I don't really feel a connection to the place. I mean the idea of living there alone, like Gloria… and doing what? Growing grapes? I don't think I could work up the enthusiasm to do it more than once. It's not like it's a passion of mine."

"Okay, back to the start. Keep your flat and spend all your weekends at the Vines. That way you'd only need to take a couple of days off work per month to have done your bit. And some months have public holidays…"

"You don't mean that, Cass?"

"No, of course not. I just hope Sue and Milo aren't thinking the same evil thought."

"I'm sure they're not. We all have similar commitments. Whichever way you split it, we all need to take four months off work over the next year, and I don't think any of us could keep our jobs on that basis."

"So it's the commute from hell or give up your jobs."

"I hate it when this kind of thing happens. We drift along happy in our routines and then something shakes us up and makes us look at life again. On the plus side, a few more drinks and we won't remember."

"Are you physically capable of working in the countryside, Liv? I'd imagine it's hard graft. Do you do any exercise?"

"Er…"

"Olivia, I worked with you at Prior Grove, remember? You used to walk a hundred yards from home to the station, a hundred yards from the station to the office and fifty yards to the sandwich bar at lunchtime."

"Right, well, I can confirm I've kept up that punishing schedule."

"I suppose you could build up your stamina over time. Have a word with Gerry and insist you go on top. That's good for the stomach muscles."

"Anyway, onto other things…" said Olivia.

Both women took a swig of their cider and Olivia gave a moment to the idea of having a different boyfriend.

No.

"Right," said Cass. "What's the definitive Kentish plan?"

"I don't know. The challenge starts in a few days. I'm sure we'll be okay for the first week or two, but after that…"

"You'll find a way."

"It's crazy, because I know nothing about vineyards and yet one is threatening to disrupt my life."

"Well, I don't know anything about vineyards either, so I can't help you there. We also don't know much beyond the basics about wine..."

"That's not true. I know a reasonable amount about wine."

"Rubbish. What you know about wine you could write on the back of a wine label."

"Nonsense."

"Okay, what sort of wine does your vineyard produce?"

"Next question."

"Do you even know how to make wine?"

"According to Google, I'm a million miles from that stage. First I have to tame the Wilds of the Netherworld."

"Name the last red wine you bought."

"What?"

"You heard."

"Beaujolais? Or was it Cote de... something?"

"I'm stunned. Such breadth of knowledge."

"Okay, so I'm no wine expert."

"Maybe you should be. Let's eat at your place. We can pick up some special supplies on the way."

"What kind of special supplies?"

"You'll see."

Half an hour later, Olivia and Cass were unpacking a couple of microwavable Thai curries and a range of miniature wine bottles.

"Ready for some tasting?" said Cass.

"Deffo."

Cass handed over the first mini bottle.

"I want you to describe it for me."

"A small red."

"Wow, I bet there are international wine connoisseurs who struggle to come up with that kind of clarity. That said, I think you're meant to open it first."

Olivia unscrewed the cap and sniffed the wine. She couldn't make out anything in particular so sniffed harder.

"You're meant to be a wine lover," said Cass, "not a drug squad sniffer dog."

"It's er…"

"Go on, what are you getting?"

"Er…"

"Strawberries? Vanilla?"

"No, just wine."

Cass took a sniff.

"Try again, Liv. I'm getting raspberry and chocolate."

"Seriously?"

"Yes."

"I wasn't joking when I said I got wine."

"Try connecting your nose to your brain."

Olivia tried again.

"Seriously, all I'm getting is wine. Frankly, if it smelled of chocolate, I'd think it was off."

"Okay, taste test."

Cass poured Olivia a glass.

"Mmm, yum," said Olivia, tasting it. "Let's mark this up as nice."

"I'm going to need a bit more than that."

"Tasty."

"You're going to be producing wine. You can't have a label on the bottle that says 'Nice And Tasty Wine'. Try again. Give me something beyond nice and tasty."

Olivia took another swig… and another… swilling it around her mouth. She swallowed and then drained the glass.

"Yes, okay, so it's fruity and tangy."

"Good, so that was an Australian Shiraz. Try to remember that aroma and taste."

"Nice, tasty, fruity, tangy Australian Shiraz that smells of wine. Got it. Let's try the next bottle."

Ninety minutes later, having finished their Thai curries, Cass opened the eighth small bottle and poured Olivia a glass.

"Are these little bottles stronger than the big bottles?" said Olivia, leaning against the kitchen doorframe.

"No."

"It's just... they seem to be tiny but powerful."

"Yes, well, each bottle is one and a half glasses. I've been having the half."

"So, I've had five glasses of big wine, but from small bottles."

"Seven, actually, plus cider in the pub."

Cass placed the glass in front of Olivia. "This is your eighth. We won't count the cider."

"Eighth?" said Olivia. "Plus cider?"

Cass filled half her own glass with the remaining wine.

"That's a deep shade of red," she said.

"I'd better give it the old sniffer test then," said Olivia prior to wafting it under her nose.

"Fourteen percent," said Cass examining the label.

Olivia lowered her glass and gathered her thoughts.

"I'm getting red berries... and red fruitiness... and red waftiness..."

"And the taste?"

"...shall remain a mystery. I cannot drink eight glasses of wine."

"Probably for the best."

For some reason, Olivia decided to sing. "Tiny little

bottles… had quite-a-lottles…"

"So what have we learned?" said Cass.

"Drink less, eat more?"

"I mean as a wine taster?"

Olivia tried to focus.

"We have learned this, Cassandra Hayley Harris… that I can't remember what the first one tasted like. How about I just walk out on my job?"

"That sounds like a bad idea."

"Yes… yes, it does. But it also sounds like a good idea. How can that be?"

"Because it can be both," said Cass.

"How long has my passion for life been dead, Cass? Like totally, absolutely dead? Because it feels like it's rising now, Dracula-like from its coffin."

"Have you decided to make a proper commitment to the vineyard?"

"I want to, yes."

"And do you think you can succeed?"

"In fairness, Cass, we shall just have to wait and see."

11

The Quote

Olivia yawned as she pulled up outside the Vines. It was just before nine and she'd been up since six. This was no way to start a Saturday, even for a part-owner of Chateau Disaster. Still, the builder would be arriving at nine.

Her phone pinged. It was a text from the builder.

> 'I'll be there at 11. Wife says I should stay in bed a bit longer as it's the weekend. Know what I mean?'

Now Ken was coming up the lane with Beano in tow. She didn't fancy talking and wondered if she could drive away and pretend she hadn't seen him. But no, this was Maybrook. You had to embrace it.

She got out.

"Morning Ken. Nice day."

"Thought about a winery yet?"

"A winery?"

"Oh, don't mind me poking my nose in. I was just curious, that's all. I expect you've worked out a plan."

"Um…?"

"About which winery you'll be working with?"

"Well, I expect we'll…" Olivia was beginning to wonder if there might be a difference between a vineyard and a winery. "Would you say we're not a winery?"

"Oh, I wouldn't know. I'm no expert at all. I did hear once that the smaller vineyards don't always have their own wineries, so they go to a local one where they can make their wine. I think Charlie and Gloria went to Ramsey's years ago, then they switched to Kirncroft's."

"Is that who you'd recommend?"

"Me? Recommend? Well, Kirncroft's are big and could be busy. I'd give Ramsey's a try, if I were you. I'm not sure if it's still there though. You could look them up on your phone."

"Ken, there must have been a harvest this year. Do you know where those grapes ended up?"

"Me? No. Kirncroft's, I expect. In fact, the whole lot might have been sold to Kirncroft's to make sure there was enough for Gloria to give to charity and pay off any tax."

As he trundled off to the main road, she googled the difference between a vineyard and a winery. Of course, it made sense when she thought about it. A vineyard grows grapes. That's it. Whether a vineyard would have its own winery on the estate was another matter. Larger vineyards had them. Smaller ones might not. She looked up Ramsey's. They weren't too far away and did seem to offer the kind of service she and her cousins would need if they were going to produce any quantity of wine.

Olivia grabbed her things from the car, including neoprene rubber wellington boots on the advice of Cass, whose husband's diving wetsuit was made of the stuff.

She entered the Vines happy that they had a lead on

wineries, but guessing it was about as practical as buying new carpets for this old place before they got the water fixed and scraped the furry green stuff from the walls.

"I'm back, Gloria. I'm thinking of dealing with Ramsey's Winery. I hope that meets with your approval?"

She wondered. What happened at a winery? Yes, you gave them your grapes to crush into juice, but then what? Did they put the juice into barrels and store it for you? Or did you take the barrels away and store them yourself?

"What's in the big outbuilding, Gloria? Do you store wine there? I'll take a look, shall I?"

She went out across the garden to the path off the far right corner. Beyond the overgrown hedge, the largest outbuilding looked as desperately sad and neglected as the main house.

Reaching the side window, Olivia tried to peer inside – but years of murk clung to the glass. There was more chance of looking through a brick wall.

She tried the door and was surprised to find it unlocked. Pushing it open was no trouble at all. It readily swung inward, only it continued its arc, broke free of its hinges and lurched sideways like a drunk to smash through the murky side window.

"Oh well, at least we'll be able to see through it now."

The outbuilding contained no wine. Spiders, yes, and possibly rats, but not a barrel or bottle of plonk anywhere. And what's more, it looked like restoring the outbuilding would cost a fortune.

Just before eleven, Olivia heard a van pull up. It was Roland the builder. He'd brought his son, who looked about sixteen. Neither of them said a lot. Roland was too busy sucking in air, tutting and shaking his head in a way that declared "this isn't good". Olivia meanwhile kept stealing glances at the boy – David, as it transpired – who followed his dad around like a puppy. Jamie would have been the same age. Would s/he have been happy learning the ropes from Alistair?

"Right," said Roland, once he'd had a good look around. "There's no point in doing a detailed costing if you don't like the ball park figure."

"A ball park figure will be just fine to get us started."

"Two hundred grand."

"Two hundred grand?"

"Give or take. A detailed breakdown of costs will take me all day and won't change the rough price I'm quoting you. The main house needs a new roof, floor joists, floorboards, new ceilings, plastering, new windows and doors, a new kitchen, bathroom, central heating system, rewiring, plumbing, painting and decorating. Then there's the big outbuilding, the smaller one, the garage, the two sheds, the drive at the side, the gardens front and rear, the patio, fencing to the front, drive gates, fencing all around the perimeter. And that's before you get started on replacing the older vines."

"Yes, well, I won't argue. What you say sounds about right. Over the next few years, we're going to do all of it. It just won't be in one go." Olivia had no idea if they'd do all of it or any of it. She just wanted to keep on Roland's good side. "Where would you suggest we start?"

"The main house roof. Then work down."

"A new roof sounds expensive."

"If I were you, I'd get permission for a loft extension. The cost will be offset by the fact you were going to spend money on a new roof anyway, and you'll gain a bedroom and a shower room."

"That's a very good idea. Um… I'd offer you tea, but

we don't have any water. Or tea."

"Is the water not on?"

"No, there was a leak."

"Where?"

"In the loft, I think."

"Do you mind if I take a look?"

"Be my guest."

Olivia showed him the stopcock. A moment later, they had water cascading down the stairs.

"Hang on a sec…"

He ran upstairs… leaving Olivia with the son, who looked mildly awkward.

"You've got a leak," Roland called from somewhere above.

You don't say. "Can you stop it?"

There was no immediate reply, but a few moments later, the water stopped cascading.

"I've isolated the tank," he said, before coming down the stairs. "It's rusted through underneath. Luckily, there's tap in the loft."

"Great, so…?"

"So now you have mains water to the kitchen sink. That's drinking water, so you're okay there."

"Is that the only tap we can use?"

"Yeah, the tank serves everything else."

"Right."

"You could fill the toilet cistern with a watering can."

"Brilliant." *Well, relatively brilliant.* "How much do I owe you, Roland?"

"For turning a tap? Nothing. It's not London, you know."

"No, well, thank you so much."

"Don't forget me when you want this place put right. You'll find my price fair and my work good."

Olivia thanked him and David for coming out on a Saturday morning and waved them off with a promise to look into getting the planning permission and finances together. In truth, she didn't know where it left them.

She texted Sue and Milo with news of the 200k price tag on putting the place right. She wanted them to have time to ponder the cost of putting the business straight, should they succeed in complying with Gloria's will, and should they decide to do it up to maximize profits when they sold it – assuming they wanted to sell it.

After sending, she read back over her text, pausing at the phrase 'put the business straight'. And that's what it was. Not a dream, but a business. Like selling used cars or lobbying government officials. A business.

12

Vineyard Viv

Sue texted back that Milo was driving them down and that they wouldn't be there for another hour or so... and that 200k was a lot of money.

Olivia went out into the garden and then beyond among the vines. It was so quiet. So absolutely still. She closed her eyes. This was a place for meditation. She'd never bothered with it before, but here... yes, meditation. Clear the mind. Enjoy the silence. *You are at one with nature. At one. Still your breath...* The peace of the deep countryside enveloped her...

"Hello!"

"Argh!"

Olivia waited for her heart rate to return to sub-critical before addressing the man looking over the fence sixty feet away.

"Hello," she said, as cheerfully as possible.

She headed closer for a more sociable introduction.

"I'm Olivia."

"Cameron. Friends call me Cam."

He looked mid-sixties and reminded her of Harrison Ford, but with no hair and a Kent accent.

"I don't know what you've heard, Cam, but I inherited the Vines from Gloria – along with my cousins, Sue and Milo."

"Yes, she said she'd try to keep it in the family. What on earth did you all do to upset her?"

"Um…?"

"Just my little joke. I expect you'll be out there pruning soon."

"Yes, I expect so. If we can find some clippers or whatever."

"Gloria kept secateurs in that shed over there."

Olivia followed his finger to a hellishly gruesome concrete structure with a dilapidated asbestos roof. The doors were practically off their hinges. It had probably been a garage at some point, possibly around the time of the Second World War. Now it looked ready to collapse.

"Thanks, I'll um… check it out later. Were you and Gloria friends?"

"Well, she was a stubborn, formidable woman, so let's hope she's gone to a happier place, eh? Now, about you. Are you planning on moving down here or will you sell it?"

"Right, so that's a complicated story. I'll get back to you on that once I've had a chance to catch up with Sue and Milo. They'll be down in an hour or so."

"Well, we can't stand here talking that long. I'll say bye for now. If you need anything, let me know."

She watched Cam disappear back to his own house, which seemed to be undergoing extensive renovation at the back. In fact, he didn't even go inside. Instead, he disappeared into a small caravan parked alongside the rear garden. And what did he grow in his field? Nothing by the look of it – although it was December. Clearly, there was much to discuss. For now, she decided to try a bit of pruning.

At the post-apocalyptic garage-shed, she carefully pushed the right hand door open. Mercifully, the hinges held and she was faced with several lines of shelves on the right hand wall. Nearest her were five or six pairs of secateurs. Olivia tested a couple on the nearby hedge and kept the sharpest pair.

She was soon out on the muddy, damp land, feeling cold despite being wrapped up, but also feeling warm from the sheer prospect of it all.

"Here we go then. Olivia Holmes, vineyard owner…"

She offered the sharp blades of her secateurs to the first of the vines. Then she paused… and put the secateurs in her pocket while she googled how to prune vines.

According to Vine Time, winter was the right time to see what you had. Without leaves, you could assess the strengths and weaknesses of trunks, cut back the inevitable tangles that had developed over the previous summer and check the canes, foliage wires and fruiting wires – with a view to preparing for another year of tidy canopies and free-hanging fruit.

Olivia looked down the rows of tangled overgrown vines that seemed to stretch into the next county. Basically, all she had to do was give each one a good cut back.

Had Gloria done this herself? No, she hired help because you obviously needed two or three hundred people.

Olivia put that out of mind. It was all about the vine in front of you, not the… how many were there? A thousand? Ten thousand?

Concentrate on this bloody vine.

According to Vinemaster, it was a simple matter of cutting vines planted last year to two buds above the graft, which would be around nine inches above ground. But what did that mean? Was it even in English?

She stepped and took in the wider vista. When were these planted? Some seemed younger than others. Farther on, some looked more gnarled and ancient.

She tried another search on her phone. Vine Valley said the whole point of pruning was to cut away most of the vine not required for the new growing season. You'll either be cane pruning or spur pruning. For cane pruning, you simply selected two or four shoots from the previous season and trained them along the trellis wires.

What?

You removed the other canes. New shoots would sprout from the buds on the chosen canes in spring. Your spur pruning would be on vines that retained one or two long canes – in other words, a permanent cordon along the trellis. Winter pruning was cutting back new canes that had grown along the permanent cordon to a small shoot cut back to two buds, known as a spur. Spring growth would come from the buds on the spur.

Olivia turned away and let out a growl. Since when had trimming plants turned into rocket science? She took a breath and addressed the first vine again. What the hell was a cane or a spur? What if you chopped the wrong bit off?

She searched again, this time looking for videos that a short-sighted squirrel could follow. Vineyard Viv was waiting. In the flesh – or on video, at least. This shapely earth mother was nothing like Olivia had been expecting.

"You see how I follow the growth?" Viv said.

Olivia strained to see.

"You see how we're assessing the vine's shape?"

Er…

"You see how we say no to big fat fruit-denying bull canes and skinny weaklings that might snap if you sneeze on them?"

Um…?

"We're after good canes, or at least the best you'll get on the vine you're addressing. This is the good earth, people. Put your heart into this and reap the rewards." Viv stared hard at the camera. "Are you in this for the right reasons? If not, go watch Vinemaster's videos. Here we work with love and respect."

Is this woman nuts?

Ten minutes later, having watched two Viv videos twice each, Olivia began to tug and snip, all the while not believing she was doing any good and more likely killing the plant.

When she was done, she stood back and assessed her butchery.

"Good luck, vine," she said. "I hope you pull through."

She briefly looked up ahead to remind herself of the size of the task, but quickly focused or the next vine. Here, she took it slowly, pulling and cutting – hoping she'd understood Viv's video advice to shape it for a balance between leaf and fruit growth while doing Viv's little dance and song.

"I may be just an overgrown ape,
But I do admire a shapely grape."
So please, dear Nature, please this ape
With a rich, sweet grape that's a grapely shape."

By the third vine, Olivia was getting up to speed. Two canes per vine. Cut each to retain eight to twelve buds depending on how healthy the vine looks. Also retain a further two spurs. But pay attention! You're looking to put right any mistakes in last year's pruning.

What mistakes? Help.

By the sixth vine, the dead wood she had pulled free was beginning to pile up on the alley floor. Tidying up would be quite a job, although Viv said the smaller bits could be left to mulch.

Olivia shivered. It was freezing cold and there was so much to take in. No one mentioned pruning could give you a headache, but following Viv, she pressed on and began to get her eye in – cutting out the duff stuff while looking for robust canes to produce next summer's fruit. If the ghosts of Gloria and Charlie lived on in the house, at least she'd be able to look them in the eye. Although, she would be able to do that for real if Sue and Milo discovered her frozen body slumped over a vine.

"Hey!"

Speak of the devil. Milo and Sue were by the kitchen door at the back of the house. Olivia went to greet them with news that she'd been pruning. The talk, however, soon turned to the house, its state of disrepair and what they might do about it – assuming one of them was about to volunteer to stay there on Monday at the very least.

"It does seem to be straightforward," said Sue. "We can't spend money on the house until we definitely own it."

"Sue's right," said Milo. "Spending two hundred grand is one thing we can forget for now. Two hundred quid might be pushing it."

"I just thought it was worth having a figure," said Olivia.

"Spot on," said Milo. "The main thing though is to work out how we can make the place habitable with little spend. We can't have you ladies getting pneumonia."

Olivia baulked. "Last time I checked, Milo, men could get pneumonia too."

"Absolutely. That's what I meant."

They went inside, out of the cold, although it wasn't much warmer in the kitchen.

"So who's volunteering to stay?" said Milo.

An unhelpful silence descended.

"I'll do a long weekend, next weekend," said Olivia. "Friday to Monday."

"I would volunteer," said Sue, "but I don't think it should be me just yet. I mean, honestly, there's not even a working toilet."

"Oh yes there is," said Olivia, handing her an old plastic bucket.

Sue's eyes widened, but Olivia calmed her down with a fuller explanation. Sue was placated. And while she filled the bucket with water from the kitchen tap, Olivia came back to their overriding concern. Who was going to stay?

They had lunch in the Old Hall pub, which literally adjoined just that – an old hall dating back to Elizabethan times. Inside the hall was a plaque naming Robert May as responsible for the construction of the hall. A dozen of his fellow contributors were named below him, but May was the main man. In fact, an information poster said that the stream just south of the village was originally May's Brook, as it passed through May family land.

There were a few locals in the pub who seemed used to spotting the occasional tourist. Olivia made a point of saying hello and that she and her cousins had moved in nearby. That didn't appear to meet with approval.

After their sandwich and small glass of wine, Milo had

to get back to London, leaving Olivia and Sue staring at each other.

"Pruning," said Olivia.

Back at the Vines, Olivia furnished Sue with secateurs and they got back to the point Olivia had left off earlier.

"Right, what do I do?" said Sue.

"Okay, so, according to Vineyard Viv, the age of the vines can be a factor. If they're too young, you won't be at full productivity. There's a YouTube of her pruning five-year-old vines, which she says are approaching full fruitfulness."

"How old are these, would you say?"

"Good question. They don't look a lot different to Viv's."

"That's encouraging. I suppose we'll just have to keep going though, whatever the age."

Olivia looked around for the hundredth time. "Do you think we'll be done by March?"

"Why, what happens in March?"

"According to Viv, once the pruning's finished, we'll have acres of vines with their canes rising up as they grow. That means we'll have to start the tying down."

"Tying down? It sounds like a book my new boyfriend bought me, only it's not about vineyards."

Her new boyfriend? Olivia refrained from asking for details, but she clearly had more to learn about her elder cousin.

"Sue, we really need to talk about Monday."

"Yes, we do."

"Well?"

"Well what?"

"Which of us will be here?"

"Oh... perhaps we'd best get some of this pruning done before we decide."

*

Later, around eleven, up in the bedroom, Olivia slipped into bed.

"Nighty-night, Sue," she called.

"Night-night, Olivia," came a voice from another bedroom.

Silence fell. It was deathly quiet. Olivia wondered whether to put the radio on but decided it would drown out the sound of any visiting team of burglars in the garden below.

"Nighty-night, Gloria," she whispered. "Please don't haunt me. We've got Vineyard Viv helping us so we're going to get it right, okay?"

There was a creak.

Olivia was up in a flash, switching the light on.

"Hello?"

The creak sounded again. In the loft. It coincided with the wind outside. She returned to her bed and tried to get some sleep. Around half-two, she achieved it.

13

So It Begins...

Olivia opened her eyes. The ceiling above her was cracked and stained, and the paint was flaking. There was also a whiff of damp in the air. The urge to get up was strong, but not just because of the state of the room. Sunday had come and gone and this was no ordinary Monday.

She dressed quickly, went downstairs and lit the coal fire. Then she washed herself at the kitchen sink before making some tea and toast.

After breakfast, she took to Gloria's chair in the lounge and contemplated whether ghosts were real.

"Gloria? Are you there?"

Silence.

Good.

Although... it would have been fun to chat with the old girl. All those stories of yesteryear.

A knock! At the front door. An actual knock at the front door.

Oh my...

Olivia gathered her strength and went to answer, although she stopped short of opening up.

"Hello?" she called nervously through the cracked wood.

"It's Ken from across the lane."

"Oh Ken…" Olivia opened the door to behold Ken and Beano. Beano was on the long leash, squeezing out a quick spray of urine over a small weed.

"I was just passing," said Ken. "Thought I'd check on you. Like I did with Gloria."

"Thanks, Ken – I'm fine."

It felt so strange. So un-London. There, you could be dead in your bed for three years before the people next door even considered you might not have gone away on holiday.

"So all's well?" Ken asked.

"Yes thanks. Fancy a cup of tea?"

"No, I'm just about to walk Beano and I'm guessing you've got a lot of pruning to get through. Next time, eh?"

"Next time then. I expect deepest Kent keeps most people busy."

"No, this is the sleepy old countryside, Olivia. Nothing much happens here."

Back in Gloria's chair, she shivered. It was going to be a cold day outside. Best wrap up warm. She glanced at the clock on the wall. It was ten-past-nine.

There was something she was meant to do. Something important.

Oh shit! Email Henry to ask for the week off!

She fired off a request on her phone. He replied almost instantly to begin an exchange.

'Is everything alright? Days off should be booked in advance.'

'Sorry, Henry. Emergency thing with builder. Don't ask. Sorry again.'

'Do you need a whole week for that?'

'Really sorry, Henry. Will explain on my return. Thanks.'

'Next time, book in advance.'

'Thanks again.'

Olivia flopped back in the chair. She lived in two different worlds now. There was no crossover, nor could there ever be. Transferring from one to the other needed planning. Perhaps she could change outfits in a phone booth...

At least Henry had been okay about it. Shaz would have said no.

But how long could you live two existences before the extended rubber band in one yanked you all the way back or the magnet in the other pulled you forward forever?

Working from home on a laptop flared briefly before the idea headed for oblivion. That would never wash with Prior Grove.

Her phone pinged. It was a Facebook post from Sarah, a friend from way, way back. She had tagged Olivia.

'Look what I found, Liv.'

The screen displayed a photograph. It took a moment, but she was soon transported back almost thirty years. It was herself, Sarah, and two boys.

'Clacton-on-Sea. Remember?'

She recalled they only spent four or five hours there. Mind you, half a day was ample time to get your fill of Clacton. It was possible to do it in half an hour.

To be fair, it had been fun.

'Remember that café with the bad menu spelling?'

Olivia had to stretch her brain cells to recall it, but it was there, lurking on the edge of memory...

'Liv? Fancy much rooms, omlit, and sosuges?'

'I remember the sea looked cold.'

'We should go back there in the summer. Massive booze-up. Whaddayasay?'

Meet up?

'No, sorry.'

'Oh? Could be fun?'

Olivia felt a need to loosen up and have fun, but she didn't think she'd find what she was looking for by revisiting her teenage years with someone who – in all honesty – she barely knew in adult life.

It encouraged her though. You could set aside whole worlds. You could live without recourse to massive booze-ups in Clacton. You could leave one life in suspended animation while you embraced another.

Out among the vines, it was good to see the progress the two of them had made over the weekend. They had got a fair way down the first few rows – although not as far as the thicker, older vines. It made sense to go back to the start and take on the next row of younger plants. Those older vines couldn't be ignored forever though. What had Ken called them? Reichensteiner, Müller-something, Schön-thing, Hex...Hux... and something else? Olivia was adamant that she should treat young and old alike. No way should the old 'uns be neglected.

Although...

She checked the note she'd made on her phone.

Chardonnay + pinot noir + pinot Meunier = champagne (must never call it that). Suggestion? Kentpagne?

The future?

Certainly, the more she read, the more she understood that sparkling wine was the way forward for English wine.

Back in the here and now, she reacquainted herself with Vineyard Viv's wisdom and begun to clip, clip, clip...

"You stayed then?"

It was Cam at the fence.

"Yes, I drew the shortest straw. Or, more accurately, I looked round and they'd gone."

"You remind me of Gloria. Not in age, of course. Just the sight of a determined woman tackling those vines."

"She did her bit then?"

"She had help, of course, but yes – very determined."

"Was she unpopular?"

"Not at all. She just didn't engage with people in later life."

"And in earlier life?"

"Oh well, I'm not one for gossip, but yes, she engaged with people then. Very much so. Don't say anything to Ken about it though. He doesn't like people speaking ill of Gloria."

"They were good friends then?"

"Yes, you could say that. I think after the War, they were very good friends indeed."

"Are you a farmer, Cam?" said Olivia, glancing to the field beyond his lengthy garden.

"That belongs to my brother. He lives over the other side. I'm a driving instructor."

"Oh." That didn't immediately strike Olivia as a country job – but then she realized that country people needed cars far more than townies. "Um... do you have family living with you?"

"No, I'm a solo act these days. My wife passed away a

few years ago. We had plans to develop the old place... as you can see."

All Olivia could see was a man living in a caravan, very probably because his do-it-yourself renovation project had halted at a painful time, seemingly never to restart again.

"Well, I won't keep you from your work," said Cam. "Bye for now."

"Bye Cam."

Olivia worked for a couple of hours before retreating to the house. It was too early for lunch, but her blood and major organs needing defrosting, so she tucked into her baked cheese and onion slice while the kettle boiled.

Just then, her phone rang. It was Gerry.

"Hello Liv. Okay to talk?"

"Yes, I'm on my own here."

"Good. All okay for tonight?"

"Tonight?"

"I know we said Wednesday, but something's come up."

"I'm actually away all this week."

"Away?"

"Yes, I only decided yesterday, so apologies for not letting you know earlier."

"Where are you?"

"Outside London."

"Yes, but where?"

"I'm in Kent."

"Kent? What are you doing in Kent? It's not one of those spa things, is it?"

"Kind of. It's a countryside connection thing. I get to... well, connect with nature and so on."

"Don't tell me... the place is packed full of feeble-minded people with too much time and money on their hands."

"That's not how you see me, is it?"

"Of course not. Now, when are you back in town?"

"Not sure. Probably Sunday night."

"Okay, well let's pencil in next Monday then. It'll have to be up my way, unfortunately. I've got a lot on. I'll pick you up at Stanmore Station, six-thirty. We'll have a nice Chinese and..."

"Okay, I'll see you then, Gerry."

"Right, well, have a good week meditating or whatever it is. Actually, what is it?"

"Yes, there's plenty of meditating... and getting covered in mud."

"Yuck, it sounds horrific. Bye then."

Olivia made some coffee and got back to her half-finished lunch. Yes, a vineyard afforded plenty of thinking time along with the mud. And that would be handy, because she had much to think about.

14

So It Continues...

The rest of the week went by in much the same way. A cold, breezy morning, both outside and inside the house, thanks to the draughty windows. A leisurely breakfast of coffee, porridge and toast followed by the call of country life and long hours in the field. She also managed to get the broken roof tiles, cracked glass panes, dodgy plumbing, and a few floor joists and boards sorted via Roland, thanks to Milo and Sue contributing alongside her.

On Saturday morning, Sue came down for the day. For Olivia, picking her up from the station, it felt like a cause for fireworks, flags and a brass band.

"It's just to give a bit of support," Sue explained.

"There was no need, Sue. I'm fine on my own."

"There's no need for every day we do here to be solitary."

From the way she said it, Olivia suspected Sue was after a reciprocal arrangement.

By mid-morning they were out on the land, pruning

alongside each other. Olivia shared what Cam had told her about Ken having had some kind of meaningful connection with Gloria, and how it was a sensitive matter.

At lunchtime, they went inside to make sandwiches.

"It's good of you to come down," said Olivia, getting the bread from the cupboard, "but you mustn't make a habit of it. It's a long way to travel and we can't all commit to doing more than our allotted time."

"It's no trouble. I was at a loose end. To be honest, it's nice to have a purpose again. Outside of work, I seem to be stuck doing endless silly hobbies just to pass the time."

Olivia was about to speak, but sensed that Sue had more to say.

"Loneliness is a funny business. I suppose really it's just a state of mind. As long as you make the effort, you can avoid it."

"Are you okay, Sue?"

"Yes, I'm fine. Keeping busy, that's the thing. Since my husband passed away, that's what I've done – I've kept busy. There have been times though where I seem to stop amid all the activity. And I wonder how is it possible to feel like there's a great big hole in your life when you've made every effort to fill it?"

"I don't have any answers, Sue. Sorry. If it helps to talk though, please do."

"One morning, I went up to the National Gallery in Trafalgar Square. While I was admiring the Constables, I found myself beside a woman of my age comparing the famous Hay Wain with its less known counterparts. Stratford Mill, for me, she said. And I agreed wholeheartedly. A much more engaging painting. Well, we discussed the pros and cons of it all for a good two minutes before she moved on. And it occurred to me that I'd enjoyed that conversation more than any other during the past few years. And so, staring at Stratford Mill, I started to cry."

"Oh Sue…"

"I'm sixty-four and I have no-one to discuss the Hay Wain and Stratford Mill with. So I thought – what the hell. Do I not exist? So, I left the gallery and took a taxi to London Bridge Station. And, well… here I am."

Sue put her arms around her cousin and squeezed.

"You want to talk about Constable? I'm your girl!"

There was a knock at the door. It was Ken.

"We were just about to make some lunch," Olivia told him. "How does a sandwich and a cup of tea sound?"

"Well, I'm off to the pub for lunch. I wondered if you ladies would care to join me."

It took Olivia and Sue two seconds to exchange a look and nod.

On the way into the village, Olivia found a way to broach a subject that had been on her mind all week.

"Were you and Charlie good friends, Ken?"

"The best of friends, yes."

"He and Gloria must have had many happy years in Maybrook."

"Most of them would have been happy, definitely," said Ken.

"Did you know Charlie and Gloria when they first moved here?" Sue asked.

"Of course I did. They only lived the other side of the High Street. It was all very happy, whatever anyone else tells you."

"I'm sure it was," said Olivia, wanting to know more – much more – but guessing this probably wasn't the time.

They passed the Old Hall pub over on their left, instead making for the Royal Standard a little farther up on the right. Olivia looked up at the sign – the Standard being that of the Royal Family, with its grand design elevating it above the coats of arms of lesser nobility.

Inside, they were greeted by two elderly men at a table.

"Hello Ken. Brought trouble, have you?"

Ken introduced Olivia and Sue to his friends, and to landlady Annie, a smart, ruddy woman of around seventy with a neat auburn bob.

"Just my usual for me," Ken told Olivia before taking a seat with his friends.

"Yes... of course."

"Don't worry," said Annie. "I think I can remember what Ken has."

"This looks sort of familiar," said Sue. "It wouldn't be where Gloria held her wine launch party all those years ago?"

"It would be," said Annie. "We knew Gloria and Charlie for many years."

As they ordered sandwiches and drinks for themselves and Ken, Annie stared harder at Sue.

"Yes, I remember you now."

"You do? It must have been thirty-five years ago."

"No doubt about it. I was telling you about the one-legged man with the two daughters...?"

Sue gasped. "My God, now you mention it..."

"Well," said Annie, "he didn't move in with the lady who ran the post office, like I said he might."

"No?"

"No, it turned out he had some family money, so he bought a half-share in a local estate agency. And as for his daughters..."

Olivia was dumbfounded. Annie had restarted the conversation as if Sue had only popped out to the loo.

It made her think though. Were they just returning visitors? Or could they become part of this world? It wasn't easy to settle on an answer.

Once Annie had brought Sue up to date, she moved on to their plans for the Vines.

"I've heard about the conditions of the will. I suppose the question is will you be selling it at the first opportunity or will you be staying?"

"I think we're looking to sell it," said Sue.

"That's not for certain," said Olivia. "It's a long way to go and who knows. The main thing is we want to treat the old place with respect while we're there."

"That's nice to hear. Maybe you'll get the bug, like Charlie did."

"Were you good friends?" Olivia asked.

"Yes, although I wasn't so keen on their wines. Mind you, that was a long way back. Techniques have improved since then. You only have to try the house wine I serve here. Back in the seventies and eighties, you would've paid good money for wine as good as that."

"So you never stocked their wine?"

"Of course I did – but just a few bottles in friendship. I couldn't afford to be lumbered with hundreds of bottles of below average wine from grapes nobody's ever heard of."

"I was here," said Olivia. "That last time she held a launch party. I must have been nine. I remember Gloria floating around in a sky blue dress. I don't recall seeing Charlie though."

"No, well, I think they were apart at that time."

"Right..."

"They soon got back together though. It was just one of their little hiccups. Charlie was a lovely man, straightforward and funny – came from a good farming family, he did, but... well..."

"A bit of a roving eye?" said Sue.

Annie moved in close and lowered her voice.

"No, it was Gloria with the roving eye."

Then she stood back again to resume their open chat.

"Charlie was a dreamer. It was him who started the wine growing. They went to a wine convention thing in the sixties and met the chap who got English wine going. Can't recall his name—"

"John Edginton," called Ken from the midst of a conversation with his friends twenty feet away.

"Yes, John Edginton," said Annie. "Anyway, Charlie was won over and Gloria went along with it."

"I quite like that Charlie was a dreamer," said Sue. "It sounds romantic."

Olivia didn't say anything. She was still amazed at Ken's supersonic hearing.

"Yes," said Annie. "The only problem was Charlie never understood how a vineyard would be sheer bloody hard work. He had this thing about being able to sit in the sun, straw hat on his head, a glass of his own wine, sipping as he looked out over his own vineyard."

"Dreamers, eh?" said Olivia, wondering if she might be in danger of becoming a dreamer too.

"Gloria tried to keep it going but struggled," said Annie.

She moved in and lowered her voice again.

"The place was on its last legs until Ray got involved about twenty years back. Then they finally started to produce better wine."

"Who's Ray?" Olivia whispered.

"An old chap who helped out. Gloria knew him from way back."

"I'd love to meet him," said Olivia.

"Oh, he died after the last harvest. Overdid it, see. Loyalty to Gloria and all that."

*

After lunch, Olivia and Sue strolled back to the Vines. Outside the front gate, Olivia paused. There was no coat of arms like at Raglington Hall. No oil paintings inside. No family history.

"Do you really think we can occupy this place for a whole year?" said Sue.

"I'm sure we can," said Olivia, pushing the gate open. "We just need to focus on producing a decent crop. That's all that matters at this stage – not our pain or difficulties. After that, we'll produce the wine and make our decision."

They went inside.

"What do you think of Gloria?" said Sue. "Do you think she was nuts?"

"It doesn't really matter what I think. Jo's certain it's all legal."

"Yes, of course. Have you thought of buying someone else's share?"

"Pardon?"

"I just wondered if you'd thought of buying someone else's share."

"I don't have the money, Sue. Besides, you want to keep your share, don't you? It's not like I could run the place on my own."

"No, I suppose not. I'm just finding the pruning hard work."

"We'll all hang on in there, Sue. Then it'll make you a nice retirement pot. You'll soon be having fab vineyard breaks in France, Italy, America, Australia…"

"Yes, I suppose so."

"This place needs all three of us."

"Yes, you're right. All three of us putting in a very big effort."

"Exactly."

A few minutes later, they were back into the work, cutting and snipping away without another word.

But Olivia's thoughts were elsewhere.

What's your story, Gloria? Is there anything beyond an anonymous life spent in an anonymous house? I know more about Sir George Raglington than I do about you.

Half an hour later, Sue stood back to take a breather.

"Do you think we're making good progress?" she asked.

"I'm sure we are."

"I'm thinking this is a lot of back-breaking work. If we're already falling short, we won't meet the harvest quota."

"I think we're alright, Sue, so let's not worry. We'll get through the pruning, collapse into a sweaty heap and then think about the next phase."

"When will that be?"

"At this rate, we'll be pruning until February."

"That's a lot of winter days outside."

"Yes, but, if we're still alive, we'll have the tying phase to look forward to. According to Vineyard Viv, you have to carefully bend each cane to the fruiting wire and tie it off with a fine wire. If the fruiting wire doesn't take the weight of the grapes, the canes could snap off in the wind."

"Well, it's sounds like interesting work," said Sue.

Olivia tried to smile. Pruning wasn't at all interesting, and the next stage didn't sound any less dull. But Sue was clearly already carrying doubts. And they were a long way from February, let alone a harvest late next year.

"What if it's not that good?" said Sue.

"What if what's not that good?"

"The wine we make?"

Olivia laughed.

"Sue, unless it puts us in hospital, it will be the greatest vintage we'll ever taste."

But then she stepped back from her own joke. She wanted very much to do this properly. Jo the solicitor would accept a bottle of fizzy plonk, but Olivia was beginning to dislike the idea of spending a whole year doing back-breaking work just to make a bottle of undrinkable grog.

Milo came down on the Sunday morning. After coffee and croissants, and a video session with Vineyard Viv, he joined them outside with secateurs.

"Jaz was trying to be helpful,' he said, while clipping.

Olivia was interested to know what Milo's partner had come up with.

"About the vineyard?" she asked.

"The house mainly," said Milo. "She gave me the name of a very chic interior designer. Apparently, muted tones are in."

Sue scoffed. "I don't think we're ready for that yet, Milo. Couldn't she come down and help with the pruning?"

"It's not allowed," said Olivia.

"It wouldn't matter if it were. She's got a coffee morning planned with friends."

Olivia drew back from judging Milo's girlfriend, who was obviously a young woman with a decent income. Why shouldn't she enjoy a Sunday morning latte with friends?

"Bloody hell, this is boring," said Milo.

"Only another five thousand to go," said Olivia.

"Are we sure we can't pay someone to do all this?"

"The only help we're allowed is at harvest time," said Sue.

"Yes, I know that. I was just wondering if we could sneak in a few unofficial workhands. They could wear disguises – you know, cover themselves in vine branches so they blend in."

Olivia laughed, but not heartily. It worried her that Milo had done almost nothing before talking of giving up.

"I know what we need," he said. "More tea."

Olivia watched him head back to the house. This wasn't the kind of commitment they needed. If Milo took up his quota of house-sitting, that was one thing – but he'd need to work damned hard while he was the tenant.

"These secateurs are blunt," said Sue. "Is there a thing to sharpen them?"

"There might be something in the shed," said Olivia, having no idea what they might need to look for.

All the same, they headed off to find out.

"All okay, Sue?"

"Yes, of course. I hope I wasn't being negative earlier. It's nice having something worthwhile to do over the weekend."

"Didn't you say you had a boyfriend? Maybe you could have gone out for lunch."

"Yes, Hugh – but… well, I met him on a senior dating site and, between you and me, I'm not sure I've chosen very wisely."

"Oh?"

"I'm quite lonely, you see, so I thought it might be a chance to meet someone nice."

"And Hugh isn't?"

"Oh, he's alright, I suppose. It's just that his main

interests seem to be watching football on my television and eating the meals I've cooked for him. And then, well, the other side of things is either quick or non-existent."

"Why don't you ditch him?"

"I don't like to be unkind."

"Right, well, I think we need to work on your pest removal technique, Sue."

In the shed, they couldn't find what they were after – whatever a secateurs sharpener looked like. There were more boxes down the end though.

Sue went to check... and screamed as something flapped around her head. This started off more flapping. And more screaming. And stuff falling like snow.

"It's alright, Sue, it's only pigeons."

Sue looked up. "There's bloody dozens of them."

"Yes, and they've had a good old clean out of droppings by the look of it."

"Oh gawd..."

They went outside for a better look at the dusting over Sue's head and shoulders.

"Hello ladies."

Sue jumped. Olivia turned. It was Cam at the fence.

"Everything alright?"

"Sue, this is Cam, the nice man who lives next door."

"Pleased to meet you, Cam," said Sue. "Just let me brush this pigeon shit off then we can shake hands."

15

The Season of Goodwill

Arriving at work on the Monday morning, Olivia spotted Laura in full flow with three others. On spying Olivia though, Laura's chattering ceased in a gear-crunching switch to mundane work matters.

"What that's, Laura. Some juicy gossip?"

"No, of course not."

Bored at the prospect of endless tittle-tattle, Olivia diverted straight to Henry's glass fishbowl office.

Henry saw her coming. She knew this because he suddenly became fascinated by his phone, no doubt already concocting some feeble fabrication concerning an important email from Shaz or possibly even the President of China. Not put off, Olivia waved cheerily as she reached his door.

"Henry, can I have a word?"

Henry looked up from his phone in surprise.

"Ah Olivia, you're back. What can I do for you? Only, it'll have to be quick, I'm in the middle of an important email from Shaz."

"I won't beat about the bush. Has there been any movement on the restructuring while I was away? In particular, as it relates to my job?"

"Nothing's decided, Olivia. It's just preliminary thoughts at this stage. Any actual plans are in the earliest possible stages."

Olivia went straight to her desk, saying hello to those she passed. Once seated, she applied for a couple of jobs on her phone. All the while, she couldn't stop thinking about the Vines. How would she be able to commit enough time there if she got a new job? She was looking at spending four of the next twelve months in Maybrook. No employer, especially a new one, would give her the time off, so it would mean commuting. Of course, if Prior Grove got rid of her, they would have to pay her off. That might keep her going for a few months. Then again, she had been getting on well with Shaz. She'd done that boring job for her and had managed to reconnect Prior Grove with two former clients. Maybe Shaz would remember that when choosing who to let go. Maybe her future was secure and stupid Henry was just a slug in the garden she would have to tolerate.

Unless…

Wasn't she a wine-grower now?

If only.

She checked her horoscope. It was quite concise.

'Go for it!'

Olivia sighed. How exactly did you 'go for it' when you'd never gone for it before?

Of course, Olivia Holmes, wine-grower sounded great. Well, someone had to stroll around those sunny vineyards, tasting and selecting the grapes for the wines that would fill the shelves at the local superstore. And it certainly beat the endless swirl of shadowy public relations. Didn't she owe it to herself to go for it? Or was that just escapist daydreaming?

Zara was coming over.

"Heard the while-you-were-away news? Shaz won't be making the decision on who to fire."

"Oh?"

"She's handed the whole thing to Henry."

Henry? Great.

After work, Olivia met Gerry in the northwest suburbs for a meal at a Chinese restaurant and time in his car – although she declined the latter. He promised he'd take her away for a few days somewhere nice as soon as he got some things straight. But how could she spend time away with him? She needed every spare day to be spent at the Vines. She started to tell him but backed out. She would tell him next time though. As an experienced businessman he'd have some good ideas on how she might proceed.

The following day, around mid-morning, Henry emerged from his office. From her corner, Olivia spotted his arms seemingly raising themselves aloft automatically.

"Attention everyone," he cried.

Oh God...

His announcements to the entire office were gaining in frequency as Prior Grove geared up for the Christmas festivities – i.e. lots of massive booze-ups, embarrassing photos, and then a week off to regret it all before returning to work full of New Year resolutions that would never see the light of mid-January.

"Management is a tricky business," Henry proclaimed,

"so to simplify things, I want you to think of Mad Max. I want you to think of Prior Grove as the group of people trying to get from that place they started out to the place they were trying to reach using resources such as steampunk trucks."

Olivia checked her nails.

"Are you playing Max?" queried Laura.

"Only for the purposes of this message."

Giles raised a hand.

"Are you playing him as in the old Mel Gibson films or the rebooted version?"

"Didn't his wife take out a restraining order against him?" said Zara.

"Henry's wife?" gasped Laura.

"No, Mel Gibson's."

Olivia scratched her eyebrow.

"Okay, forget Mad Max. The thing is… certain elements are going to be merged, job-wise. That will mean difficulties as we travel down the job-merging road."

Olivia's heart thumped. Word of Shaz was finally coming down via Henry and it was unlikely to differ from Word of Shaz coming down via the firm's army of gossip-merchants. All the speculation was exploding into a hard reality. Her job was going down the drain and her only salvation would be applying for any kind of job now. Literally anything. It was that or go to Kent and stay there.

Kent…

She thought of talking to Henry in private. He could dispense with her services on the spot, hand over the eight grand severance payment and they could shake hands.

"Nothing's been decided yet," Henry continued. "I'm

just going through the best ways to make this work. I only thought it fair to forewarn you. I'd rather this was kept out in the open. Shaz and I dislike gossip. On the positive side, we're probably only looking to lose eight or nine posts from the joint offices, so possibly only four or five from here."

Goodbye Prior Grove.

Perhaps she would laugh about all this come the summer. She could see it now. Sitting in the sun, a straw hat on her head, a glass of wine in her hand, lazily surveying her vineyard.

Her phone pinged. Could she attend a job interview on Friday?

"Olivia?"

It was Henry. A personal summons.

She followed him to his office, where he failed to offer her a seat.

"Right, well," he said. "I'm meeting Shaz in ten minutes, so let's get to the point. As an exercise, I'd like to challenge you to come up with a cost-effective method of reorganizing the teams in a way that would preserve your job."

For a fleeting moment, Olivia brightened. Henry was trying to help her.

Or was he...?

"Um..."

"Let me repeat that," said Henry. "I want you to come up with a cost-effective method of reorganizing the teams in a way that preserves your job."

Olivia frowned.

"Isn't that management's job?"

"We've tried. Without success. See if you can come up with something creative."

Great, so if my job is cut, it's my fault.

"Show me you're dynamic, Olivia."

"I'll try."

"Shaz wants to see your commitment."

"My commitment... right."

Olivia tramped back to her desk wondering how the hell she was meant to go about taking on such a poisonous challenge. Maybe tea would help? No, a cup of cool, refreshing water.

Only... someone had stolen the water cooler. Surely, that had to be a health and safety issue.

Then she spied it.

"What the...?"

Somehow, possibly due to an overnight earth tremor, the water cooler – that magnetic focal point of conversation – had slid thirty feet down the office to stop just short of Rob's desk. That is, Rob's raised desk. Indeed, Rob's raised desk that now boasted a tray on the edge nearest the water cooler. A tray containing cookies under a sign that proclaimed 'Please Help Yourself'.

What was the little twit up to? Okay, so he'd have an endless stream of visitors and okay, he'd have every female in the office thanking him once an hour for the cookie they were munching.

He was dressed differently too. A darker suit with a crimson and black tie.

He was still talking the same crap on the phone though.

"...yes, well, I'm introducing a pop-up approach to research strategies..."

Olivia took her water, but no cookie and headed past the busy Giles and Zara to the sanctuary of her desk.

Sipping water, she aimlessly read an email. Being fired had always seemed a vague event, but it now was a-coming like a frickin' express train. It was obvious Henry didn't expect her to come up with a solution. What he wouldn't expect was for her to come out of her corner firing magic spells like Harry Potter.

Across the office, Rob was sharing something funny on his phone. Of course, he went all the way to Henry with it. Busy Henry found the time to chortle along with him.

Well done, Rob. You're safe.

Come Friday at 11 a.m., Olivia was walking into an interview full of hope and trepidation. Fifteen minutes later, she was leaving in a confused state. Seemingly, Henry had been cloned and was now the assistant director in every bloody public relations office in England. Certainly, the dipstick interviewing her had touched on key assets such as commitment and passion being essential to the corporate side of public relations. Olivia had found herself assuring him that after ten years in the business she was in a fair position to know what was needed.

Leaving their offices, she decided she would commit to the countryside. The redundancy money would keep her afloat for a while and they would look into claiming any agricultural grants that might be available, assuming fizzy wine was considered an essential crop. Also, Gerry would be persuaded of the need to halt their sessions for the next year – which would give him time to sort out leaving his wife. Then, once the mission had been brought to a successful conclusion, they would put the Vines up for auction. Her share of the sale price, after auction costs, would be around eighty to ninety thousand. Then she would sell her flat, pay off the mortgage, and have around two hundred grand. With Gerry matching that from one of his many accounts, they would be able to buy a four hundred grand flat for cash and have no mortgage to worry about. That would mean less pressure on her in terms of earning a big salary and they could consign unsatisfactory venues for their encounters to the dating dustbin.

It was a good plan. A solid plan. And it began with her being let go by Prior Grove.

I'm going for it. I'm bloody going to run a vineyard. Yes! Freedom here I come.

Zara texted.

'Prior Grove emergency over. New business partner. No job losses. Shaz said THE BOARD HAVE DECIDED TO KEEP EVERYONE ON.'

What?

'WE'RE A TEAM OF WINNERS! ALL DOWN THE PUB LATER!!!'

But I'm leaving…

Christmas Eve-*Eve* meant leaving work early to buy a couple of presents. A book for Sue and some aftershave for Milo. Then it was straight up to the northwest outer suburbs to meet Gerry.

Over pizza, she told him about the Vines and showed him the photos.

"Well?" she asked when he fell silent.

"Sell it."

"I've already explained – I can't. Not just yet."

"I cannot believe those conditions. What a vindictive

old bat."

"She was no such thing. I think she was lonely and let that affect her judgment. I'm learning she was quite a complex character, which is good when you think she never existed for me, and yet now she…"

Gerry's head was shaking.

"Forget all that. Getting eighty to ninety thousand next year is brilliant. You could do a lot with that kind of money."

"Yes, I was thinking we could go fifty-fifty on buying a home for ourselves."

Gerry raised an eyebrow. "Yes… yes, I suppose that's an option. Another option is to turn that money into a real fortune by investing it wisely."

"Oh?"

Christmas Day came in cold but dry, and Olivia woke up to zero presents – as usual. No doubt Gerry would belatedly remember to buy her something in the sales.

She thought of Jamie. This year it would have been clothes she bought for her son or daughter. Well, when they're teenagers, what do you get them?

Then there was the shared present. The one she got for the whole family. So, with Alistair gone, and Gerry with his wife, that was just her and Jamie. It was – as always – a jigsaw puzzle. One thousand pieces.

This one featured a pastel painting of a seaside picnic, with a happy family sitting around a gingham cloth laden with all kinds of food and drink. The backdrop was green pastures and blue sea, and of course, blue sky. This would require a bit of thought and Jamie's help would definitely be required. No sneaking off to hang out with friends, my precious lovely daughter/son. No-one should be alone at

Christmas.

Oh Sue...

Olivia got dressed, bagged up all the Christmas stuff she could, and headed for the car. On the way, she thought of texting her cousin, but decided against it. She wanted to surprise her, and that was something she'd never done before, to anyone, ever.

She was surprised herself when she reached the Vines. Milo's car was outside. His girlfriend was at her parents, so he'd come down to make sure Sue had a proper Christmas dinner. It was a brilliant gesture and Olivia was suddenly proud of her young cousin. This is how her Jamie would have acted, she hoped.

The Christmas dinner they had together was the best Olivia could recall. They had a bit of everything, wore silly paper hats, and played silly party games. And they swapped presents. Olivia was delighted with her bath time bonanza pack from Sue and fully-lined garden gloves from Milo; Milo was very happy with his aftershave from Olivia and aftershave from Sue; and Sue was beside herself with her fluffy slippers from Milo and giant illustrated hardback of John Constable's life and works from Olivia.

At one point, Milo and Sue started discussing dating disasters. Olivia felt like she was trapped in an episode of Love Island. She wondered – could they create a functional family from the disparate entities of herself, Sue and Milo? Well, perhaps not as cousins, because currently she was living in a sitcom as the mum, with Milo the cheeky son and Sue the dotty granny.

Then Milo proposed a toast.

"To the Vines!"

A cheer went up. Quite a big one, in fact. They had only been in residence for three weeks, but something was evolving.

But Milo wasn't finished.

"And to the money we'll get when we sell it!"

Another cheer went up, although this one was smaller.

16

Commuters

Late in January, early on a Monday morning, Olivia's eyes sprang open. She'd heard the alarm – yes, loud and clear – but had somehow drifted off again.

Crap!

Having now overslept by thirty minutes, she leapt out of bed and started dressing on route to the bathroom, tripping over her half-on uncooperative panties and the uneven floorboards. Breakfast went south and she was quickly in the car driving to the station six miles away. This would come down to a matter of seconds. This she knew because she'd made the station run a few times already. Since New Year, she and her cousins had been sharing duties and commuting. All had complained, but what else could they do?

At the station, someone had brought their fleet of cars with them to take up all the spaces. That meant driving back hundreds of yards to find a space by some houses that were probably inhabited by people who moaned about commuters' cars blocking up their street.

Olivia burst out of the car, hit the pavement and ran – possibly threatening a number of British sprint records.

At the station, she rushed through waving her pass and hit the platform – which was empty because everyone was aboard the train which was about to move out.

She hit the door button, almost had a heart attack when nothing happened, and then nearly passed out with relief as the doors belatedly slid open to admit her.

On board, she looked around for a seat – without success. It would be an hour on her feet on the slow train to town.

At London Bridge, she switched to the Tube – Jubilee Line to Westminster; District Line to St James's Park. Then it was a short walk to the office in Buckingham Gate, where she sought out the restroom for a mini-collapse and full freshen-up.

At her desk, Henry moved in fast. Passion and urgency were needed for a truly terrible client revolving around making immense profits on building new executive homes on parkland. It was a big commitment that would involve long hours of cajoling the local authority to do its bit in overhauling the UK's lamentable progress in building new homes for poorer people.

Olivia wondered if commuting was a good idea. Yes, legal eagle Jo had accepted that she could commute and still be resident at the Vines. If she was doing some work there before or after her commuting, then it was in order. The terms of the will didn't specify an exact amount of work they needed to put in each day, just that they had to meet a harvest target. Although, if Olivia lived there and didn't prepare enough vines for production, then they risked losing the task and the vineyard.

That said, she hated commuting with as much passion as she was hating the project Henry had dumped on her –

72 luxurious, expensive new homes plus eight lower cost homes for social inclusion reasons. Of course, the cheaper homes would be high density with a separate entrance.

Later that day, around eight p.m., she was standing in a Kentish vineyard, pruning with a light strapped to her head, wondering if she was in danger of losing her sanity.

Saturday morning, Olivia was in bed, staring at the cracked ceiling, as still as a stone, while her brain struggled to juggle things. Alongside her, Gerry was snoring gently. In the previous weeks he'd been going on about all the things she could do when she sold her share of the vineyard. He felt she should invest the money in a business. She'd make a pile. Still, it had been good of him to venture down to Kent on the Friday, even if his eight p.m. arrival and desire to try the Chinese restaurant in the village hadn't exactly fired her exhausted mind or body.

She kept wondering what kind of business she might invest in. A cake shop sounded fun. She could learn how to bake great cakes and sell them to people like herself. It had disappointed her that Gerry didn't grab her idea of going fifty-fifty to buy a nice little property to live in. It had been yet another reminder that she shouldn't rely on him doing the right thing by her.

There was the other idea, of course – that she could stay on at the Vines. Its appeal seemed lop-sided though. On the smaller side, a grape-growing and wine-making business. On the other, decades of standing in fields while life passed her by. Not that Prior Grove protected her from life whizzing by.

She wished she could be someone else. Someone who could take their ten years of experience in pushing the agendas of others and use it to create a business. But she lacked the passion and commitment for a business in the area she knew.

She checked the clock. It was just after six-thirty.

By nine, she was accepting Gerry's brief bout of thrusts. By ten, they were having coffee prior to him going back to London for a weekend conference.

"I've been thinking," he said. "Why don't you bring your business plans forward?"

She didn't understand. "How?"

"Sell your interest in the vineyard early."

"I can't. I don't own a share. Not until we've met Gloria's conditions. I told you all that."

"Yes, but you will meet those conditions if you have money."

"Are you offering to buy me out?"

"Me? No. I was thinking Milo sounds the kind of young man who would gobble up a chance to boost his money."

"You've lost me, Gerry."

"Look, let's say you'll walk away with eighty grand in eleven months' time. So what you do is sell your share to Milo today."

"I still don't understand."

"You'd have to offer him a carrot. Say a discount of fifteen grand. That means he buys you out for sixty-five on condition that you work here full-time to meet the conditions. He's freed of any obligation to spend his time here and he'll get more than his money back when he and Sue sell up."

Olivia took a sip of her coffee. It sounded like a plan. Or at least the kernel of a plan. But was it one she could get behind? Working at the Vines on what would be someone else's vineyard and then making less money than the others…?

"I'm not sure it makes sense."

"Think about it. You'd have sixty-five thousand to invest in a much healthier business right away."

"Yes, but to cut all my financial ties to the Vines…"

"It's a vineyard, Liv. Vineyards get a good year, a few average years and a few bad years. Start at the wrong point and you'll be bust before you know it. It's not worth the aggravation."

"You paint a gloomy picture."

"Look, you're in a position to earn a lot more than any discount you'd give Milo."

"I'm not sure I could work here and not be a stakeholder. Plus, I don't even know what kind of business I'd want to invest in. And I certainly have no time to start anything else, so it would hardly be ready and waiting when I finish in Kent."

"You could invest in one of my businesses. And I'd be running it for you. This time next year, you'd be worth 120, 130."

Olivia experienced a spike of excitement and suspicion.

"I'd be business partners with you?"

"Why not? We're already a good fit."

"Yes, but…"

"Think about it. You'd have enough money to pay your monthly mortgage so you'd keep your place in New Cross, you'd be getting into a new business with me thereby freeing yourself from the whims of that scummy lobbying firm you work for, and you'd be setting your cousins up for the future. You did say Sue looks unsuited to the physical challenge?"

Olivia took another sip of coffee. Put like that, it did seem a viable way of making progress.

*

After their coffee, Olivia stood at the front gate to wave Gerry off. As his car disappeared up the lane, she pondered his offer. She would become a company director – not at the Vines, but in one Gerry's companies. Would that work? She'd be free of Prior Grove and she'd get to spend a year in the countryside. It all seemed to add up.

And yet… if it all added up, why did she feel that it didn't quite add up?

She shivered. It was much colder than she'd imagined. Back inside the house, she went up to the bedroom to grab another layer of clothing from her bag.

What would Alistair have advised?

Her ex-husband, looking relaxed in a T-shirt and jeans, appeared on the bed – fully reclined, hands folded behind his head on the pillow, feet crossed.

"Break it down," he said.

She studied his golden hair and hazel eyes – and dismissed his charms.

"Into what?"

"Into what you have. One, a job you're comfortable in but not in love with. Two, a chance to part-own a vineyard, even though you know nothing about grapes or wine…"

"I do know about wine. A bit. And I've done a ton of pruning."

"Three, you have a hefty mortgage on your apartment which makes the idea of losing your job a bit scary."

"My job is safe. Prior Grove has a new partner. They'll be rebranding soon. It's a rosy future."

"They could change course, seek to slim down – you

know that."

"Right, well, if we stick to the mortgage payments, we both know who walked out demanding a pay-off for their half of our joint investment…"

"Four, at some point, one of you might fall sick and you'll fail to fulfil the occupancy requirement."

"Please don't say that."

"I suppose you wouldn't lose this place if Jo never found out."

"Jo has spies. She must have."

"Who."

"It could be anyone. And everyone. It's a small community."

"Five, Gerry's plan would take away any money worries. Assuming Milo wants to make a killing. The downside is you'd become a manual worker for most of this year. Manual work is hard."

"So that's it, laid out."

"There's one other variable."

"Which is?"

"Gerry. Can you trust him?"

"I don't want to discuss that with you."

"He hasn't even said what kind of business you might be investing in?"

"He's into business advice. He has some big clients."

"Who?"

"I don't know. He has to sign non-disclosure agreements. I do too, remember?"

"What if he runs off with your money?"

"That, Alistair, is exactly the sort of thing I've come to expect from you. Do I make snide comments about Sophie?"

"It's Stephanie, as you well know."

"Alistair? Go away."

Alistair vanished.

She trusted Gerry. She had to. There was no-one else she could trust. Of course, people can let you down. Alistair had let her down. They had been a team, a unit, a couple. When he left after twenty years, her first reaction was to vomit over the mat inside the front door he'd just closed on his way out. The shakes then took hold as she contemplated failure and emptiness. Then the financial realities kicked in. She was going to struggle, so she'd have to ditch being cheeky at work. She'd have to knuckle down and become a model employee. Then the love she had been giving to Alistair had nowhere to go, no role, no purpose.

"Gloria?" It seemed odd involving Gloria. Even so. "How did you feel when Charlie died?"

There was no reply, but Olivia guessed there would have been the same emptiness, but with more sadness and less confusion.

Olivia shook it out of her head. This wasn't what she wanted to focus on. But it remained.

Loneliness.

What did it mean? Wasn't there a quote… something she'd read somewhere… Facebook, probably. 'Loneliness and the feeling of being unwanted is the most terrible poverty.'

Yes, Mother Teresa's words.

But was she right? Wasn't loneliness a kind of freedom? You didn't have to pick your mess up if there was no-one there to complain about it. You could do as you pleased. Not that she liked mess.

Of course, the solo life had its downside. With Gerry, she could enjoy a restaurant meal anonymously. After all, who looked at other couples? But go there alone? Every second, every forkful, every sip, and all eyes would be on her. She would fuel speculation at all the other tables. Who is she? Why is she alone? Has she been dumped?

Loneliness happens to people. But to fight it at any cost? Did that make sense?

Okay, so she didn't love Gerry. She needed him, though. He made her… un-lonely. And she guessed by throwing his business offer back at him, she might drive him away too.

Alistair reappeared. Stephanie was straddling him, bouncing up and down to satisfy her needs.

"Stop that!"

Stephanie huffed and vanished. Alistair was still there, fully dressed and seemingly unaware of the pleasure he'd just been experiencing.

"There's one other option," he said.

"Oh?"

"Why don't you and Gerry buy out Milo and Sue?"

"What?" But her surprise was half-hearted, because she'd had a vague notion along those lines. "Go on…"

"Well, Gerry could buy out Milo and Sue, and then you could stay here, maybe Gerry too for the occasional weekend – anyway, you would complete the conditions of the will, take control of the property… and then, you could either sell it or you and Gerry could restore the place to glory and live here happily ever after."

Olivia pondered that. She didn't want to force Milo and Sue out, but if they weren't committed…? It scared her that one of them might abandon their house-sitting duties and lose the task for all three of them. Who could she trust? Okay, so they were family – but only just. Really, she hardly knew them.

17

Commitment

Around half-eleven, Milo and Sue arrived – he'd brought her down in his car to save her the train fare. The strain of commitment showed on Milo's face though as soon as they joined Olivia among the vines.

"I need to get out of my upcoming week," he said.

"Oh?"

"Sorry, it's a work thing."

"I can't get the time off work," said Sue. "The odd day is my limit. There are already raised eyebrows."

"I'm really sorry," said Milo. "I'm definitely still committed. I mean I have to be. Ever since I told Jaz, she's not stopped going on about selling the Vines, getting the cash and us heading off to Miami for a month."

He donned gloves to help with the pruning.

"We need to cover next week," said Olivia. "I have one more day of annual leave left. Then I have to wait until April."

"The school closes for half-term at the end of

February," said Sue while clipping. "I'm supposed to go in for a couple of days, but I could probably get the whole week off."

"Let's cheat," said Milo. "Who would know?"

"We would know," said Olivia. "And I'm sure Gloria would know."

"That's nuts," said Milo. "It doesn't change anything though. We still need to find a way to cover more days."

"I'll do more then," said Olivia. "I'll commute full-time. That means an hour's pruning before I go out and an hour when I get back – ten hours Monday to Friday, and I'll be living and sleeping here. Any days you two can do, you just show up and get stuck in."

"That's an amazing offer, Liv," said Milo.

"Unless…" Olivia hesitated. "Unless we go for a more drastic approach."

Milo looked intrigued. "Such as?"

"Well, it's just an idea, nothing more, but what if one of us bought another of us out?"

"Go on," said Milo.

"I don't understand," said Sue. "Do you mean you want to pay one of us off? I mentioned that a while back and nobody thought much of it."

"Time has moved on, Sue. I'm not saying it's a great idea, it's just that if one of us isn't into this, they might want to cash in early."

"Sounds like you've been giving it some thought," said Milo. "Could you afford it? We're talking eighty to ninety grand apiece."

"If I sold my flat I'd be able to pay one of you off. I'm just trying to find a way to guarantee we cover the coming year. At this rate, we'll fail and get nothing."

Sue frowned. "But if you commute like you said…"

"I'd do it to save the inheritance, Sue, but it has to be a

last resort, doesn't it? You wouldn't really stand back and let me do it solo, would you?"

"There are too many options at the moment," said Milo, "and not many of them mean anything. At some point we need to whittle them down."

"Prune them?" said Sue, pleased with her pun.

Milo ignored it.

"The only sensible option at the moment is for Liv to commute for the next few weeks to save the inheritance. All the other stuff… we need to discuss. I could pay off one of you, if I can raise the money… one of you could live here full-time and the other two pay their bills… or, like Liv said, she could sell her place in New Cross and pay one of us off."

"It all sounds complicated," said Sue. "Maybe the three of us should just try a bit harder. With a bit of luck, we'll get through the year intact."

"That's what I'm saying," said Milo. "All the options go on and on but none of them can take shape yet. I say we stick to Plan A. That's Liv taking the reins for a few weeks, then it's Sue's week, then mine. In the meantime, we keep looking to find the one best way."

Milo and Sue looked to Olivia.

"I'm hating it already, but…"

"Well done, Liv," said Milo. "You're a star. We'll keep thinking up options. We need an ongoing dialogue. Update and tweak, kind of thing. No pressure, no drama – just never losing sight of the main objective."

"So, for now, it's still the three of us," said Sue.

"Yes," said Olivia. "All for one and one for all. Now let's get some pruning done."

"The Three Musketeers," said Sue, grabbing a rough-looking twig and pulling hard… and it snapping, sending her stumbling back two steps before gravity took over and landed her rear end in the mud with a thump.

"Rhubarb, anyone?"

It was Cam at the fence, holding up a handful of pale, slender stalks.

Olivia helped Sue up.

Milo waved but continued pruning, leaving Olivia and Sue to approach Cam to learn how he grew his stalks in a warm, dark shed to get a steady supply from the last days of January through to early March.

Olivia felt pain at watching Sue try to pull her wet clothing out of her crevices.

"Have you tried it forced, Sue?" Cam asked.

"Tried what forced?"

"Rhubarb. That's what we call it when it's grown in the dark."

"Er, yes, I must have," she said.

Olivia felt that Cam looked a little awkward. Maybe he wasn't used to women with mud-covered nether regions? In some parts of London, people paid good money for that kind of thing.

"It's a local variety," said Cam, seemingly keen to talk – mainly to Sue. "Perfect for forcing. If you grow it in the dark, it creates stems that etiolate or grow pale. It's photosynthesis that makes them green, so we stop that by shutting out the light."

"It sounds a bit cruel," said Sue.

"It's having the plant desperately reaching out for light that gives us sweet, pale stems."

"Yes, well, we ought to be getting on," said Sue. "I've got a soggy undercarriage to sort out."

"Righto," said Cam. "It's not really cruel though. To rhubarb people, it's the king of the early crops."

"Thanks Cam," said Olivia, accepting the bunch of stalks on behalf of them all.

Once out of his earshot, Olivia nudged her elder cousin.

"Well, well, Sue…"

Sue huffed. "I'm not interested."

"In Cam or the rhubarb?"

During the afternoon, Olivia broke off pruning duties to stroll to the village to get some milk, bread and other basics. Her walk took her out of the lane and past the petrol station on the other side of the road.

She crossed to say hello to the man who ran it. She'd done this three or four times since taking over the Vines. He never did more than grunt a response, but Olivia wanted to get to know everyone who lived or worked nearby. If… and it was only an if… but *if* she decided to stay on, which was far from likely, then she wanted to be part of Maybrook and not just some outsider living apart.

Before she got there, the sound of whistling reached her ears. Andrew Lloyd Webber. The song from *Cats*. What was it called?

Memory?

She walked past the fuel pumps to the workshop. The big double doors were wide open and the whistling was coming from the back of an old Ford hatchback.

She moved around it to find the garage owner on his knees at work. The rear wheel was off and he seemed to be doing something with the brakes.

"Cats," she said.

He looked up at her and then all around.

"Where?"

"No, the song. Have you seen the show?"

"What show?"

"Cats."

"Can't say I have."

He resumed his work.

"It was on in London for years," Olivia persevered.

"I haven't been to London in years. Last time I was there was for my sister's wedding. She married a bloke called Sam Riley. Do you know him?"

"Sam Riley from London? No."

"Just kidding."

"Pardon?"

"Just playing the country dimwit." He stopped his work to address her. "I believe London has about ten million people. You would have been within your rights to tell me that. But you didn't. You assumed I was dim. That's called being patronizing, by the way."

"Right, well... I've learned my lesson. I only stopped by to say hello."

"Hello then. And could you hand me the WD40?"

Olivia looked up to where he was pointing – a shelf bedecked with an array of cans and pots. She knew her WD40 though. When she was little, her dad swore by it.

She handed him the can.

"Something stuck, is it?" she asked.

"That's right. A drop of this'll loosen it up nicely."

"I'll be off then."

"Righto."

"I'm sorry if I came over as patronizing. I don't know many people here and hope to put that right. I just got off to a bad start."

"On the contrary, you know what WD40 is. That's a good start."

"Oh, you mean because I'm a woman I wouldn't normally know what WD40 is? That's called being patronizing, by the way."

"Well, I reckon you're right. Let's call it evens."

He got up and offered his hand.

"I'm Gus."

"Olivia," she said taking his hand – and regretting it as she could feel the oil and grease transferring to her own.

"Right, well, I'd better get back to it" said Gus.

"Yes, don't let me stop you. And do please whistle. You hold a tune really well."

"You think so? It drives some of my customers mad."

She left Gus behind but heard his whistling all the way to the bend that took her into the High Street.

A little farther on, she stopped outside the Old Hall pub, and ventured around the side to stare at the old hall itself. Then she crossed the road to take a look at the church. It was quite small, possibly many centuries old, with an aging clergyman weeding the lawn at the side. But it wasn't meant to be a leisurely stroll – mainly because there was pruning to do – so Olivia bought the few bits she needed and headed back.

Opposite the petrol station, she halted… and then crossed the road to seek out Gus once more. He was putting the wheel back on.

"Just a thought, Gus," she said. "If you ever need help, a part-time assistant for your paperwork or anything…"

"No, I don't need any help, thanks. I've got it all covered."

"Right. Just thought I'd ask."

Olivia got back to the Vines to find Sue and Milo on a tea break in the kitchen. They were discussing family. Olivia made herself a cup and broke open a packet of chocolate digestives she'd bought. Sue, meanwhile, was being surprisingly positive in trying to fire up a flagging Milo.

"If I can do it at sixty-four… and look at Olivia.

Forty-four. And there's you, twenty-four."

"Twenty-five. It was my birthday last week."

"You never said."

"Don't worry about it."

Olivia knew how he felt. She never made anything of her birthdays. Far better to just let them float by.

"Well, you have a family now," said Sue. "Sending cards is part of that. At least, it should be."

"Yes, well, there you go – I don't place the same value on family as you do, Sue. For me, family let you down. You rely on them too much then you lose your mum to kidney failure and your dad to prison."

"Oh..." said Olivia, in surprise.

"At least you'll get Dad back," said Sue.

"I don't want him back."

There was an awkward silence.

"How long did he get?" Sue eventually asked.

"Fourteen years."

"That's a long time," said Olivia, worrying about what he'd done. None of the crimes flooding her brain were particularly reassuring.

"He was in financial instruments," Milo explained. "Derivatives, securities and so on. He was greedy though... illegal channels. He cost a lot of people a lot of money."

"Has he got long left to serve?" Olivia asked.

"No, he got out after seven."

"He's out?" said Sue. "How is he getting on?"

"No idea. I don't have any contact with him."

"So, he's not a relative of Gloria's then?" said Olivia, thinking of the will and its beneficiaries.

"No, that was my mum."

Sue sighed. "Well, perhaps there's *some* family you can trust. No need to bracket Olivia and me with your underhand father. I work in a school and I'm sure Olivia's work in public relations is squeaky clean."

"Moving the subject on," said Olivia, "is there any objection to the three of us sharing my extended commuting costs?"

"No problem," said Milo. "We're all in this together… until we aren't."

Sunday morning's dream of being loved by Gerry in a huge four-poster bed was interrupted by Gerry – on the phone.

"I've been thinking," he said.

"Me too," said Olivia, now staring up at a familiar cracked and yellowed ceiling. "Do you have a four-poster bed?"

"What?"

"At home. Do you have—"

"Liv, you're taking on too much. I reckon you going solo in any business venture will affect your health. Physical and mental."

"Gerry, it's before nine on a Sunday morning. I'm trying to catch up on my sleep."

"I was thinking of your poor dad."

Olivia sat up sharply, causing Gloria's old bed to creak loudly in protest.

"What?"

"You told me he ran a small business and ended up killing himself."

"This isn't the time to talk about my dad, okay? He had a lot of issues and a lot of debt."

A vision of him polishing one of his used cars came to mind. How he made them gleam. They still didn't sell though.

"I'm just saying you need the support of a business partner," said Gerry. "If you're going to avoid all the pitfalls."

"I haven't decided what I want to do."

"I mean *whatever* you do. Think about it, okay? Think about partnering with me and all those problems your dad faced will be gone."

"I'll think about it… but not now."

She ended the call and flopped back onto the pillow.

Was Gerry right? Was she taking on too much? Hell, what exactly was she even taking on? Wasn't it time she came up with a real plan and stuck to it?

She closed her eyes and Alistair was making love to her. No! Not Alistair, Gerry.

No… not Gerry… oily handed Gus…

No, this was a time for more important things, like pondering her decision to commute longer-term if they couldn't come up with a better plan. Because sixty miles to London and sixty miles back, every day, in rush hour…

Yuck.

After a morning of pruning, they went to the Royal Standard for a lunchtime sandwich and beer.

Ken was there with advice to not spend too much time in the pub. He said they had to get the last of the pruning finished before the weather warmed up, when any fresh pruning would make the sap bleed profusely – not a good thing.

Olivia pondered what she was facing. Doing a good job at Prior Grove while doing a good job at the Vines? Was that possible? And what if she sold her place in New Cross and went into business with Gerry? Argh, the brain churn just wouldn't stop.

"A penny for them," said Annie the landlady.

"My thoughts? Yes, that's all they're worth. I might be staying at the Vines for the next few weeks. I was wondering... I mean I can't spend much on it, but it needs so many repairs. Roland the builder helped with a few things but I can't keep asking him. Do you know anyone who might be able to help on the cheap? We've still got some rotten joists and floorboards, a back door that's more rot than wood, a cracked washbasin..."

Annie considered it. "I might know someone who can help."

"A phone number would be brilliant."

"No need."

Annie called a man over. He was tall, perhaps mid-thirties... and, with short russet hair, sapphire eyes and broad shoulders...

Olivia clamped her jaw shut and hoped he hadn't spotted her drooling.

"Leo, this is Olivia. She's desperate and short of money."

Wow, thought Olivia, it's like I've signed up to anti-Tinder.

"It's house-related. We need to replace a few things. Floor joists, floorboards, a back door..."

Leo smiled. "Give me a list and I'll see what I can do."

Olivia was certain about one thing. Leo was very attractive.

No! Back to business.

"I'll write one up and leave it with Annie. Thanks Leo, it's really appreciated."

He nodded and went back to a conversation with friends.

Joining Sue and Milo, Olivia returned to their ongoing commitment.

"I was thinking we should talk though our options again."

"Really?" groaned Milo. "It's starting to feel like a circle of hell."

"I know but we have to keep going over everything until the best idea wins."

"Go on then."

"So what if I sell my share at a discount. I'd stay on full-time so you two would be free to go back to your normal lives. You could help if you had time, but there would be no commitment."

"Remind me," said Sue. "How does that benefit you?"

"It would give me options. One of them would be to invest my money elsewhere."

"In one of Gerry's companies?" said Milo.

"Possibly. The thing is it's a plan. I'm not saying it's *the* plan, but a plan to guarantee we get through this without falling short."

"Okay," said Milo, "let's say, for fun, that I'm interested. Let's say I feel no tie to the vineyard…"

"For fun?" said Sue.

"Don't complicate things, Sue. Let's just say I've raised the money to buy Olivia out. Then she would get, say, fifty grand now…"

"I was thinking sixty-five."

"Okay, it's just for fun, so Liv gets sixty-five now. Where does that leave us? Sue, you'd get eighty at the end of the year, and I get a hundred and sixty minus what I've paid Liv. So, ninety-five. These are just rough figures, but would we all be cool with that? Me, ninety-five, Sue, eighty, Liv, sixty-five?"

"I'm not sure," said Sue. "It doesn't sound fair."

"Not fair?" said Milo. "As opposed to something going wrong and all three of us getting a big fat zero?"

"Nobody wants that," said Sue.

"Why don't I see if I could get the money?" said Milo. "If I can't, then it's all academic."

"And if you can?" said Sue.

"Then it would be up to Olivia."

Olivia nodded. "It's not for certain, Sue. I just feel it's good to know which of our options are genuine. I might be fine commuting full-time to get us over the finish line. But sometimes circumstances change and life moves on. Sometimes, you have to go with your best offer. Sixty-five thousand is a lot of money and Gerry knows his stuff. I'd be a fool to overlook that."

18

Big News Bud Break

One Saturday morning in mid-March, with the pruning and tying down done, and with warmer weather on the way, Olivia began to feel a little more into her stride. She felt the others were getting a feel for it too now. Certainly, Sue's detective novels had been replaced by well-thumbed books on wine and viticulture.

In future years – if any of them were still at the Vines – they would face replanting. And that would require money as well as time. For now though, Vineyard Viv suggested a period of waiting and doing what they could away from the vines.

That gave Olivia hope she could continue commuting a little longer and that the contract Gerry had drawn up could remain unsigned in Gloria's room. Not that she had said no, but it was March and the end of the year didn't seem quite so far away now. Plus, come April, she would get her new annual leave allowance of twenty-five days. What with public holidays, and Milo and Sue's time off, there was a chance everything might yet fall into place.

Okay, so commuting was a pain, but plenty of people did it, and some of them would be doing it decade after decade until retirement. For Olivia, it wouldn't be like that. If she could just get to the end of the year, she would have eighty to ninety thousand to invest in whichever business took her fancy.

Gerry, however, was not at all happy to hear such thoughts. He couldn't believe she was dragging her feet. It wasn't that simple, of course. The idea of Milo buying her out had yet to evolve into a genuine offer because arranging unsecured finance to purchase part of a property with tricky inheritance conditions attached to it wasn't straightforward.

Olivia went to the front window, looking out for Sue and Milo's arrival. When she saw Ken and Beano passing, she went out to say hello.

"Did I mention tasting?" said Ken.

"Tasting?"

"Yes, I'm going back a few years, but they had a tasting just up the road. Some fellow came down – he was in the trade, by all accounts. Don't ask me for details. I don't recall much about it. Joshua Skelton-Jones, Master of Wine, I think he was. He arranged what they call a blind tasting. Don't ask me how it works, but the Kent and Sussex fizz stood up to some of the champagnes. They did a piece about it in the local paper. Photos and everything."

"That's amazing," said Olivia. "And encouraging, too."

"Well, I'm not surprised. The soil hereabouts is good for producing fizz with a well-balanced acidity."

"Right..." *Not that you know much about wine or vineyards.* "Do you think that was down to Ray's help?"

"Ray?"

"I heard he helped them for twenty years."

"Oh, *that* Ray. Possibly."

"Was it Ray who got them into sparkling wine?"

"I don't recall. He did get them into Kirncroft's though. A very big winery. It became quite a production by the end. Lots of terrific quantity."

Not quality?

"Well, we're a long way from wineries," said Olivia, wondering if Ken's thoughts on Ray could be relied on. "According to Vineyard Viv, we have lots to do before the new shoots start to appear."

"Yes, but you've got time. No need to bust a gut. I heard someone somewhere say when you've done your pruning and tying down, it's a good time to catch up on other things."

"Yes, I've heard that too. What kind of things do you think they mean?"

"Oh, I expect they mean things like considering how you're going to control costs, crop quality and quantity, setting up company accounts, website ideas, branding and labelling ideas, increasing your knowledge, planning new planting, making repairs to trellis and posts, taking soil samples for testing, assessing nutrition choices... that kind of thing."

"Well, Ken... you are an absolute mine of information. Next you'll be explaining quantum physics."

"What, particles that can be in two places at once and whose actions are affected by the observer? That's way over my simple head, Olivia. Don't forget to look into wineries, will you. Bye for now."

"Bye Ken."

Ten minutes later, Sue and Milo turned up in Milo's car. Olivia went out to greet them.

"Before you come in – Ken was reminding me about

looking into wineries. Do you remember that place I looked up a while back?"

"Ramsey's?" said Sue.

"Yes, anyone fancy a trip over there?"

Pulling into the car park at Terry Ramsey Vineyard & Winery, Olivia could see what a professional operation they had going on compared to the Vines. First of all, there was space for a dozen customers to park. Then there was the friendly welcome sign indicating that you could have coffee and pastries and buy wine.

The shop and café was actually part of a larger building – the winery, with dozens and dozens of barrels and containers, and countless bottles. Olivia noted that the living quarters – a lovely, large character property – was situated fifty yards away, giving the owners privacy.

And then there was the vineyard. It seemed three or four times wider than theirs, and definitely disappeared a lot farther into the distance. If the Vines was seven acres, then Terry Ramsey's place had to be twenty or more.

"Hello there, I'm Kate Ramsey, the winery manager," said a small, jolly woman, possibly in her eighties. "I won't keep you a moment."

"No problem," said Milo.

Kate was busy dealing with a customer who, it transpired, was there to taste the latest vintage now that it had been in tanks and barrels over the winter. She was concerned about the blend and when to bottle.

"This looks lovely," said Sue, eyeing up Ramsey's Number 49 Cuvee. "I might have to buy a bottle."

A few minutes later, Kate came over.

"We're looking into winery facilities," Olivia explained.

"Yes, it's that time of year, isn't it," said Kate. "The

sap is rising, the days are longer and the blood is beginning to fizz."

Olivia felt the enthusiasm. It was as refreshing as a morning shower.

"Yes, we offer winery services," Kate confirmed.

"Have you been in the business long?" Milo asked.

"Forty-odd years," said Kate, "so still a beginner."

Olivia laughed politely but suddenly felt completely outside of winemaking.

"My husband Terry and I only meant to try it as a sideline," Kate continued, "but it gets into you. Terry was ever so passionate until his passing. The rest of us try to live up to that."

"I'm sure you do," said Sue.

"So," said Kate, "what specifically are you after?"

Olivia, Sue and Milo looked at each other.

"Good question," said Olivia. "We're growing grapes and we're going to need the services of a winery. Beyond that... we don't know."

"Okay, do you know what yield we're talking about?"

"Not really," said Sue.

"Well, grape crops vary from year to year," said Kate, "but you need an idea of yield or you won't know how many barrels you'll need on hand."

"We wouldn't even know how to estimate it," said Milo.

"Well, let's see. Do you know how many vines you have?"

"We reckon it's seven thousand over seven acres," said Olivia.

"A thousand vines an acre sounds fine," said Kate. "If you're planning long-term you might want to look at nine hundred per acre to improve health and quality. Now, taking into account unknown factors like soil, weather and disease, you might expect three to four tons of grapes per acre. And let's say you'll get 150 gallons of juice per ton. This is all conservative, just to give you an idea."

"So 450 to 600 gallons per acre," said Milo.

"Yes, a barrel takes sixty gallons, so now we're getting closer to what you'll need."

"It sounds a lot," said Olivia.

"It sounds like a business," said Milo.

"Would you have room to take us on?" said Sue.

"Yes, it's possible, but you'll want to know a bit more about us before you decide where to take your business. You wouldn't put your son or daughter in the first school you passed."

"No, we wouldn't," said Olivia.

Kate went on to point out all the key features of the winery – how barrels and bottles were stored, arrangements for tasting and blending, and a myriad of other details. Olivia lapped it up. Everything sounded just right.

"Yes, it's a whole other process away from the vineyard," said Kate. "Speaking of which – have you had bud break yet?"

"I don't think so," said Olivia. "Not last time we checked."

"Ours was this morning. It's like magic, isn't it."

"I hope so," said Olivia, now desperately wanting to check their vines again.

"What did you do before wine?" Sue asked.

"This was a forty-acre orchard until the early seventies. Then Terry saw a thing on television and that was that. We turned an acre over to chardonnay and pinot noir and we haven't looked back. The vineyard now covers thirty acres."

"So you still get to make apple pie to go with the

wine," said Sue.

"Indeed we do."

"How many grape varieties do you grow?" Milo asked.

"We currently have ten. That gives us a good range of red, white, rose and sparkling. Our first wines went on sale after the hot summer of 1976. Last year we produced over a hundred thousand bottles."

"That's a lot of wine," said Sue.

"We have to stay on our toes, mind. Back in the nineties, everyone was drinking chardonnay. Then it was pinot grigio. The future is sparkling wine, we feel."

"It all sounds perfect," said Olivia.

"We do offer facilities to smaller growers and we still have some capacity. I'm sure we could accommodate a seven acre harvest."

Olivia's mind was already made up. She didn't want to go anywhere else.

On the way back to the Vines, Sue, cuddling a bottle of sparkling cuvee, was chirping happily about Ramsey's – but Olivia had an idea it was Kate, the octogenarian wine manager, who had stoked the fires of enthusiasm.

"I can see you in a few years, Sue," she said, "bubbling away like Kate."

"That's what I was thinking," said Sue. "It puts me to shame to see someone much older than me thoroughly enjoying her role in life."

That thought hadn't been lost on Olivia either.

"It's a pity we'll be selling the Vines," she said.

"Yes," said Sue. "A pity."

Milo remained silent, possibly because he was concentrating on driving them safely along the twisting, narrow country lanes. Or possibly because he wanted to get his hands on the bounty they could have at the end of the year. Or... was he calculating how much money they could make selling their wine?

Olivia took it all in – the countryside, yawning and stretching now, getting ready to do its stuff. Bud break? She hadn't looked for a couple of days.

"Well, it's been a nice family trip," said Sue, out of the blue.

Olivia smiled. Yes it had. They each had a family size hole in their lives. They could do a lot for each other, if they stuck together.

Back at the Vines, they headed straight out the back, with Milo consulting his phone.

"Look between the stem and the petiole," he said. "I guess Viv means between the twig and the stalky bit that ends in a leaf."

They watched the video that had only been posted the day before.

"Bud break," said Viv. "That's life happening right there in front of our eyes. The healing power of our Mother Earth, pushing out life so the Universe may experience itself through a trillion, trillion life forms. Some, like us, are lucky enough to observe and understand how precious bud break is. It's only embryonic, but all life will come from this."

Jamie appeared in Olivia's mind. Was he getting interested in grape growing?

"Grape growers," said Viv, earnestly, "the other great thing about being a human in charge of vines is you can make up new songs between videos. Ahem...

"My heart was aching, but now my buds are breaking,

157

The sun is up, and life is filling up my cup,
And my vines will be on time
And my time will be measured in wine."

Olivia laughed.

"And now for the happy dance," said Viv.

She danced – and she was clearly insane. But in a good way because she made Olivia laugh some more.

"Embrace life, vine lovers."

"Bud break, anyone?" said Milo.

It felt like an Easter egg hunt. The first few vines Olivia checked looked unchanged.

But then...

"Here's one!"

"Here's another!" said Sue, sounding genuinely excited.

"Four, five over here," said Milo. He even smiled.

It was a sunny day in the middle of March and buds were breaking through their protective scales all over the vineyard. Olivia felt a surge of relief and satisfaction. All that pruning and tying in freezing cold weather. And now – a tiny green bit pushes out of the thicker bit and all is right with the world.

The three of them did high fives, and then Sue and Olivia hugged each other.

After a calming cup of tea, Olivia had an urge to tell someone. Cass would be pleased. Cass would understand.

Her phone rang. It was Gerry.

"Hey, perfect timing, Gerry. I have amazing news."

"Milo's got his money together?"

"No."

"You've signed the contract though?"

"No, I'm talking about vineyard stuff."

"So am I."

In truth, Olivia had endured a crap time at Prior Grove with useless mind-changing clients and hadn't told a soul. Now they had bud break, the biggest and best news ever.

She told Gerry how it meant they were on track to produce grapes.

"That's good," Gerry said. "Grapes means wine. I'm not overlooking that. Meeting the conditions of that stupid will is vital."

"Yes, but it feels like more than that. It's... well, special."

"Yes, I'm aware how special nature is, Liv. I've seen the TV shows. The thing is, your real business opportunity is waiting for you. Have a word with Milo. Tell him to pull his finger out. And sign that contract. We may as well have all the paperwork sorted ahead of time."

Olivia let Gerry go on for a couple of minutes before bringing the call to an end. Then she turned to Milo.

"Gerry was wondering if you could do a bit more to get your finance arranged."

"I've already told you – it's not so easy."

"I know."

"One independent broker I saw must have googled down into my DNA. He mentioned my dad doing time for illegal trading. Then he wondered why I was looking to raise sixty-five grand to buy something you don't have the right to sell me."

"Ah... I see."

"I have a reputation to maintain, Liv. I mean if it all went wrong...? Also, are you really sure you want to sell up? I mean look at you. Bud break and you're dancing and almost bursting into tears. If anyone quits, it should be me."

"But I can't buy you out."

"You could if you sold your flat."

"True…"

"I still don't know what the hurry is," said Sue. "We're starting to put more weeks behind us. Why can't Gerry wait until we complete the task?"

"It's a fair point," said Milo. "We could have the deeds in nine months. What kind of plan has he cooked up that needs sixty-five grand pronto?"

Olivia sighed. "I don't know."

Later, back among the vines, they went about making double-sure the new fruiting canes were properly tied to the fruiting wires. These grapes were going to be a big part of their lives over the next few months. Thankfully Vineyard Viv showed them how to bend the cane gently so that it lies along the wire. The idea was to avoid snapping them off when doing so.

"Doing it on a dry day isn't recommended," said Viv.

"Doing what on a dry day?" said Milo.

"Milo, you are so cheeky," said Sue. "Viv says canes are suppler in damp conditions. She also says early morning's good because rising sap aids bendiness."

Milo turned to Olivia. "I hate smutty talk."

Cam appeared at the fence.

"Hello," said Sue, hurrying across, but in a way that suggested not hurrying.

Olivia and Milo left them to it. From Olivia's view of this and the past weeks, Sue was falling for Cam. She would deny it, of course.

"Love is in the air," she said to Milo. "You just never know when it's going to show up."

Her phone rang. It was Leo out the front.

"You were saying?" said Milo.

"Don't be silly."

Olivia welcomed Leo at the front door. He had eight

long, reclaimed floorboards she could have for thirty quid. She nodded appreciatively.

"Can I give you a hand?" she said.

"Olivia, I'm going to need both your hands and a firm grip."

It was ridiculous. Was the whole countryside swamped in innuendo?

Leo indicated the first board.

"Okay, grab the end," he said.

Once they had stored all eight in the lounge, Olivia invited Leo to come and see their bud break. He was instantly into it.

"This is great. You guys are going to have a really good year."

Olivia was thrilled. Leo understood it in a way Gerry didn't. It was as if she'd switched worlds.

Gerry phoned again, but she rejected the call.

Instead, she texted him.

'Having second thoughts. Bear with me. Sorry to be a pain. Big decision.'

He texted back saying she needed to act with more maturity. She could make a million in five years, then pay off her mortgage and buy her own vineyard.

Olivia put her phone away. Could Gerry really deliver that kind of success? In fairness, he already owned several businesses, had a huge house and drove a variety of expensive cars. The prospect of working with him had to be taken seriously. Unless he was a complete fraud, of course.

19

Lovers' Lane

A fortnight passed where Milo and Sue managed to cobble together a schedule to take over from Olivia in keeping the train on the track – a fortnight of normality for Olivia, where she could live in New Cross and have a relatively short commute to work, and meet Gerry in the northwest suburbs.

Now it was her turn for a week at the Vines once more, with all the joys of long-haul commuting. Still, they were at the very end of March now, which meant two things. One, Olivia would soon get a new annual leave allowance of twenty-five days, and two, Sue's school would close mid-April for the two-week Easter break, of which she could take a week away from the office.

Driving down to Kent on the Saturday morning, Olivia had time to consider how things were shaping up. Life at Prior Grove was okay. More tiring when she had to get there from Kent, of course, but not impossible. Her latest client seemingly loved her commitment to his high-end property development aspirations, in particular the way she went about targeting elected representatives at a premier London borough with her continual reminders of their responsibility to help solve the housing crisis. She had won a couple of them over by helping them onto a vote-attracting 'I care' platform – always a good approach with elections looming. Henry said he was putting her work for the developer on a more permanent footing.

One thing that had been giving her pause for thought was Leo. They hadn't had any contact while she was in London and there were no plans for any kind of meet-up. She just felt something.

She still respected Gerry, of course. It was just their latest meet-up had been a real bore. Not that Leo was offering anything. It was just that feeling. And she knew he knew because when two people exchange a certain kind of look, they know.

But that was part of the downside. Having spent twenty years with one man, she didn't wish to become free and easy. She just wanted to find the right partner and get back to being a woman who was loved and cherished by her man. It wasn't too much to ask, was it?

Had she chosen wrongly in Gerry? No, she didn't think so. Her divorce from Alistair hit her badly and Gerry was the rock she clung to. When they first met, he spoke the right words, he offered stability, direction and hope for a settled future. He took her out to dinner and away for weekends. He smiled and listened. He told her all the things she needed to hear and it helped at the time. However, the fact remained that none of the promising words he'd uttered on their joint future had ever looked like coming to fruition – until now.

Now he was offering a chance to be in business with him. That wasn't to be rejected out of hand. Gerry had a large detached house in the northwest London suburbs and several fancy cars. Would he be okay about parting as lovers but going into business together?

Although, did she really want to join one of his businesses giving advice to other businesses, when she had no interest in that area? That said, staying on at the Vines would also be her taking on a business that she had very little experience in. She was learning, yes, but they were still just out of the starting gate. There was a lot of track ahead and it might be more than just a little bumpy.

She switched her thoughts away from business for a moment. The weather was good, the road was clear, and she was heading for Kent and, possibly, Leo.

Or was that just a dream, an idyll, a fancy. He was a decent country boy at heart but he had to be seven, eight years her junior.

Maybe she was asking too much.

Leo…

Encourage? Or steer clear?

No sooner Olivia arrived at the Vines, she was having a cup of steaming hot tea and a slice of buttered toast with Sue. And before they were halfway through, Ken came knocking and accepting an invitation to join them.

"Them canes behaving themselves?" he asked.

"Yes, all good," said Sue.

"None of them brittle then?"

"No… I don't think so."

"No sign of disease?"

"No. Viv warned me about phomopsis," said Sue, "but we seem to be okay."

"Phomopsis?" said Olivia, realizing she hadn't kept up with Viv's videos.

"I wouldn't know much about that," said Ken, "but I suppose any kind of fungal disease would be a problem. Glad to hear all's well."

After their tea and toast, Olivia and Sue strolled into the village to get some provisions. The prices were a little higher than New Cross Sainsbury's, but Olivia didn't mind if it supported the local community,

On the way, they crossed over to say hello to Gus.

"How's business?" he asked.

"Slow," said Olivia.

"Well, good fizz can't be hurried."

"How about you?"

"Slow."

Something occurred to her.

"Do you ever sell secondhand cars?"

"No, why?"

"I just wondered."

"I do get the occasional old banger. It's not a line I want to get into though. I mean this is hardly the place for it. I'd have to move to Maidstone or Canterbury. Even then, you might not make money."

Olivia thought of her dad struggling to sell old cars in London. She was glad Gus was on the ball.

"Did you know Ray?" she asked, getting back to wine.

"Ray?"

"He used to help Gloria with her fizz. I was told he died after the last harvest."

"Oh, you mean Raymond," he said, emphasizing the second syllable to make it sound Continental.

"Ray-*mond*?" said Sue. "Was he French?"

"Yes, Raymond Lafayette. I used to look after his Renault. Came over as a boy during the War. Nice man."

Olivia reconfigured the character of Ray into Raymond.

"Was he a vineyard expert?" she asked.

"Yes, he always said he saw England as an extension of France. The downs and the white cliffs of Dover? He told me that strip of soil goes under the Channel and comes up in France – all the way down to the Champagne region. It's less than a hundred miles south of here, apparently. Similar weather, too, so why not make the same wine? That was his thinking. It's just they won't let you call it champagne."

"And he and Gloria weren't…?"

"No, I don't think so. Then again, I'm not into gossip. Otherwise I'd be asking Sue how she's getting on with Cam."

Sue raised a brow. "Me and Cam?"

"I know it's none of my business," said Gus, "but he always mentions you when he stops by. Sue this and Sue that. You'd think Olivia and Milton had nothing to do with the place."

"I think you mean Milo," said Olivia.

"Milo, yes, that's the one. Not got his heart in it, has he."

"We don't know that for sure," said Sue protectively.

But Olivia felt sure.

Later, back at the Vines, Sue seemed distracted as they finished their lunchtime toasted sandwiches. Olivia didn't like to ask her to stay over till Sunday. She had done her stint and there wasn't any need for her to stay – beyond companionship.

"What time might you be leaving, Sue?"

"I'm not sure."

"No problem. The trains go at five past the hour, don't they?"

"Yes, so we've just missed one."

"Well, whenever you're ready, I'll give you a lift to the station."

"Actually... I'm just popping out. I won't be long."

And Sue was gone, almost in a flash.

Olivia went to the front window and watched Sue turn the wrong way for the village, but possibly the right way if you wanted to knock on Cam's door.

"Sue, you old rascal."

As it was, Sue was gone for seven hours. When she returned, she looked flushed and exhausted.

"Sue?"

"Well, I've never yakked so much."

"Is that what they call it nowadays?"

"Talked, Olivia, talked. Cam is such a lovely man. And quite lonely too."

There was a knock at the door. Olivia answered it to find Cam there.

"Oh, Cam. Hello?"

"Hello, Liv. Is Sue in?"

In? You've only just...

"Yes, of course." She turned and called out. "Sue?"

Sue came to the door and so Olivia got out of their way by going into the kitchen and pretending to do some tidying while straining her ears to the point they might burst.

"I'm such a twit," Cam said. "I was dying to ask you to go out some time, but I couldn't get the damn words out."

"I'd love to go out."

"Really? How about now? We could pop into the village. There's that nice Chinese restaurant."

"Now? Er... I'm not quite dressed for it. Um... half an hour?"

"Great. I'll meet you here then."

Sue came back inside liked a disturbed hen.

"What did Cam want?" asked Olivia.

"Oh nothing. We thought we might pop out for a bite to eat."

"A date?"

"No, more two friends having a meal. I'm done with relationships. They're unreliable. Did I tell you about Ben from that dating site?"

"Ben? No. You told me about Hugh."

"Ah well, there was a Ben, too – he was just the same. Cam and I will be friends, that's all."

But Olivia had heard the eager tone in Cam's voice.

"Sue, I don't think Cam just wants to be friends."

But Sue was too busy getting herself up to the bathroom to discuss it further. And, half an hour later, she was too busy blustering out of the house and down the path with Cam, village bound.

Silence fell once again at the Vines. Olivia was alone, although happy to be so. There was much to think about. What to do about Gerry on two fronts: relationship and business. And what to do about Leo on the single front of should she or shouldn't she.

"Well, Gloria, what do you think? Sue and Cam? Will that work? Come on, answer me. You had some experience. You would know."

Gloria...

Still something of an unfinished jigsaw puzzle.

She had started out as a ghost, a nothing... and then there had been the video, which gave nothing away. But people are people. They have lives. Sometimes lives more extraordinary than we might know. And yet lives, however varied, that are lost to us, and to history, so that it's like they never really existed.

But Olivia had some pieces.

Gloria, young, a cheeky teenager with a couple of admirers. Ken and Charlie. This ghost had been a woman, and she deserved to come back – not in the flesh, but where she belonged, in people's memories. What did people say about her? That she was a formidable woman? Well, there weren't enough of those in the world. This one should be remembered. Faults? Yes, she may have had one or two, but so what? Who were the faultless who could point a finger? Olivia didn't want to know them. No-one was faultless.

20

Deal Or No Deal?

The following morning, Leo phoned with news of a house being renovated – that is, gutted with all its innards thrown out. He could get the cousins some reclaimed materials.

Olivia was keen because Leo seemed to know his stuff.

"You'll have to come with me," he said. "I'm not offering you anything unless you really want it."

Sue was fine with that. She had things planned with Cam, who had also volunteered to drive her to the station later. Olivia imagined their parting would be like that scene in *Brief Encounter.*

Ten minutes later, Olivia was enjoying the short trip in the flatbed truck Leo had borrowed from a friend in the trade. There was something about being in a big, basic work vehicle as opposed to a small, comfy car. Trucks carried people with a sense of purpose – even if the purpose was just to get some timber. Maybe Leo saw the flatbed as a big badge that said 'Outta my way, I'm a worker'. Or maybe he didn't.

At the property – a big, half-gutted detached house that looked like an old rectory – Olivia and Leo worked up a sweat bringing doors and doorframes down from the upper floor. She liked the way he could handle heavy weights. She couldn't imagine Gerry doing anything like it without having a heart attack. This was like a return to Alistair when he was younger. He loved physical work. He used to say it put him in the mood.

Next they measured up kitchen cabinets that looked only a few years old.

"These'll do nicely in your kitchen, Liv."

She agreed. They would. And, as he began unscrewing the first of them from the wall, she thought about those times with Alistair… and thought how that might be with Leo.

Two hours later, they had a full load.

"How about a quick beer to clear the dust from our pipes," said Leo.

"Okay."

He drove them back to Maybrook and pulled up around the back of the Old Hall pub.

"Better parking here," he said.

Olivia guessed he meant compared with the Royal Standard opposite, where there didn't seemed to be room for larger vehicles.

Getting out of a truck felt good. She even slammed the door because it felt right. Leo might not be seeing the truck as big badge that said 'Outta my way, I'm a worker', but Olivia damn-well was.

A small boy looked up at her in awe. He was with his family. Early tourists, come to see the Old Hall.

"Built in 1604," Leo told them. "Make sure you go round the back. There's some steps up to a balcony.

You'll get some great photos there."

The family thanked him, but veered away from his boorish, door-slamming co-worker.

In the pub, armed with a beer and a sandwich, Olivia found herself telling Leo some of the things she had done in life. A separate part of her wrenched itself free to observe, and then reported back to her that, yes, she was acting like a high school girl trying to impress a guy.

"So, Leo. How about you? What makes Leo tick?"

Why am I talking like this! Get a grip, girl!

"Me? I'm just me," he said with a casual shrug. "I get on with things. But let's hear more of you. What do you make of the countryside now you've been here a while?"

"Well… I suppose I'm looking to find a way in and a way to be at ease. I'm hoping the countryside will accept me."

"Oh, the countryside will accept you. Most definitely."

There was a certain way he looked at her. She understood it. She smiled at him, enjoying the attention, but if she couldn't allow him into her life, could she? Wouldn't it be too much upheaval while she was trying to make sure they didn't lose their inheritance? On the other hand, this was the countryside. This guy was a country boy. Big and strong, and yet kind and thoughtful. She thought of living in London with Gerry and helping him run a business. Or leaving Gerry but staying with Prior Grove. Then she thought of making love with Leo and being part-owner of a Kentish vineyard. And the answer?

She wondered. Would the Vines ever be about getting paid at the end of each month or receiving a company dividend? Did it really offer something that could get into her head and heart? It had fields and flowers and birds overhead. It had sun and rain. And right now it had Leo. Wasn't this the life she wanted? What would Alistair say?

What would Gerry say? Or Gloria? Or her blessed Jamie? Or would she wake up in the morning and see it differently?

After their lunch, they took their haul back to the Vines. Sue was next door with Cam, but Milo was there to help unload. Leo didn't hang around once the back of the truck was clear though. He had to get it back to his friend.

Ken came along after a while to see what they were up to. He was without Beano, who was unwell with some unspecified ailment. After a cup of tea, they went out among the vines, where there was a definite hint of green taking hold.

"I see the buds are producing shoots," said Ken. "You can't beat that greening of the view."

"We might have to start mowing the alleys soon," said Milo.

Ken seemed very upbeat. As if the new life in the vines was something you could co-opt into your own system.

"I've seen these alleys in many a spring and summer," he said. "Daisies, buttercups, eggs and bacon, bluebells, blue bugles, sneezewort..."

He seemed to drift off. Olivia wondered if memories of years past were coming back to him.

"We've got that patch up the back," said Olivia. "Charlie's little nature reserve. I'm looking forward to seeing that grow."

"The jungle? Yes, you'll have all sorts thriving in that."

A shadow flashed over them. Olivia gazed upward.

"An eagle!"

"No, that'll be a kestrel," said Ken.

And that's when it hit Olivia. This life in the countryside, with all its trials, it offered moments like this.

The sun rising higher in the blue and drying out the land. The air filled with sweetness. Little birds flitting around the vines and the hedgerows. And above, a kestrel hovering and then striking to catch...

"A mouse!" gasped Olivia.

"A vole, by the look of it," said Ken.

"A vole then."

Olivia was transfixed. This wasn't park life, this went deeper. Deeper into the land and into the spirit. This wasn't something you came to see. This was life itself.

"Careful," said Milo. "You might never want to leave."

"Maybe you won't have to," said Ken.

"I haven't decided what to do," said Olivia. And that was still true.

"I'm sure you'll make the right decision," said Ken. "But I'd better be going. You've got things to do. I don't want to get in the way when you're spraying weed killer."

"Is that the thing to do?" Milo asked.

"I've heard people mention carefully spraying a narrow strip under the trellising. I recall Charlie out with his backpack sprayer. He was always careful to do no harm beyond that strip. Nature first, he used to say."

After Ken left, Olivia found the spraying equipment in a shed and worked out there was at least a day, possibly two of this to come – once they had bought some weed killer.

Around mid-afternoon, Sue popped back. She was going to stay on a bit for a date with Cam.

"Where's Milo?"

"He's over at Ken's changing a light bulb."

Sue smiled.

"Restaurant, is it?" Olivia asked, putting the kettle on.

"Yes, the Italian place."

"It'll be lovely."

"It's funny how food plays a role in relationships. You remember I told you about Hugh? It was as he heaped in the third or fourth forkful of spag-bol, that it dawned on me. Those daydreams we all have... he didn't feature in any of them."

"And Ben?"

"Him neither."

"And Cam?"

"All I can think of is Cam and me curled up in his bed. I hope that's not too shocking, Olivia?"

"No, it's lovely. I'm jealous."

"I'm just worried about how best to impress him."

"What? You don't have to do that."

"Am I worldly wise enough?"

"Sue, it's Cam. He grows flippin' rhubarb. You do not need to read Cosmo or Fifty Shades. You just have to be yourself and possibly express an interest in rhubarb."

Sue laughed. And Olivia smiled.

"You have such a lovely laugh, Sue. It draws people in. It's genuine. Er... but don't laugh too much – he'll think you're nuts."

"You mean don't force it like his rhubarb."

They both laughed.

"Do you think Cam could be long-term," said Sue, suddenly serious.

But Milo came in and so they switched the conversation to weed killer.

Six p.m. brought a surprise. Gerry turned up. He'd texted earlier to see how Olivia was doing, but now she could see it had been a ruse to make sure she was in residence. He wanted some privacy from Sue and Milo, so Olivia invited him out among the vines.

"You can see it's greening up now," she said.

Gerry nodded and mumbled something vaguely positive but moved swiftly on to other matters.

"What's happening with Milo?" he asked.

"Milo?"

"We had a plan that he'd buy you out."

"It's not going to happen, Gerry."

"This is the best opportunity you'll ever get, Liv. Offer him a bigger discount. Tell him it's his for fifty grand."

"Gerry, it's almost April. Six months from now, we'll have completed the harvest. Then we'll only need to produce a bottle of fizz…"

"Liv, this is a serious proposition. I drew up that contract specially. I'm guessing you still haven't signed it?"

"Why would I sign it?"

And for the first time, she felt something rising. Like the sap in the vines, there was a source of energy flowing through her.

"I'm not selling the Vines, Gerry. I'm keeping it. At least I'm going to try to keep it. I need to give it two or three years to know if it's the life for me. You don't give up on an opportunity like this to invest in something you know even less about."

Gerry grabbed her arm.

"Look, I need that money. I'm practically on the point of divorcing my wife and I have to push through a business deal hard and fast in the worst possible conditions."

"Can you let go of my arm, please?"

He did so.

"Look, tell Milo he can have it for forty. He should be able to raise that."

"Forty? You haven't listened to a word I've said."

"You'll treble it in a year. Guaranteed. A big opportunity has come up and I need to move fast. Sell your share to Milo."

"I don't want to."

She felt a surge of power, which set her pulse racing. Gerry didn't react well.

"This is a business decision, not some stupid poetic affair of the heart. You need someone with business experience to work with. Me."

"Then why don't you buy out Sue and Milo? Then we'd be together, running a vineyard."

"This is not the kind of business I'm talking about."

"Then we're not on the same page, Gerry. I'm not saying I'm mad keen on being a vineyard owner – yet. I'm just saying I need to give it a fair try. Surely, you can see that?"

"I need you to… I need your help. If you don't invest, we'll both lose out big-time. This time next year, we could be married."

"Married?"

"Yes, would you marry me?"

"Is that a proposal?"

"If you want."

Olivia was flustered. "I don't understand. Why don't you re-mortgage your house or bring another partner in. There must be other business people out there. Maybe an investment bank could help? Once they've seen your figures…"

Gerry's face didn't flinch, there wasn't even a fraction of flicker, but Olivia sensed something.

"I'll tell you what, Gerry. You send me all the financials. All the facts and figures relating to this. I've seen those shows on TV where business people invest in newcomers. I know how it works."

"You wouldn't understand the figures."

"No, but my lawyer would. He's mustard when it comes to deals."

"What lawyer?"

"My cousin… Milo."

Gerry wasn't happy, but he said he'd put some figures together and get back to her. She was wondering how to put him off any idea of staying the night, but she needn't have worried, because he was away in a hurry.

Standing alone in the field, with the light fading, she recalled her dad running a small business and killing himself. Was Gerry right? Was his way the best way? Or had her new life begun?

21

April Showers

A week passed with Sue and Olivia making a pact to take turns commuting. One of Olivia's nights had been the Wednesday. Leo stopped by, but the house felt too isolated to have him there. She had to be sure this time. Her gut feeling was that she and Leo could become something and that this country life could be everything she had ever wanted. She just didn't want to spoil it by putting a foot wrong. So she sent Leo away on the basis that she had to go to bed very early in order to get up very early. She promised him some time at the weekend, if he was interested.

Leo was very much interested.

Arriving at the Vines on the Saturday, Olivia was welcomed for mid-morning coffee by Sue, who had stayed over on the Friday night. Half an hour later, Milo turned up looking tired.

"What a week," he complained. "Long nights at the

office. A big client."

Olivia understood all too well. Then Milo brightened.

"I've invited Jaz down," he announced.

"Oh, that's good," said Sue. "I'm sure she'll be impressed with what you've achieved.

"What we've achieved, Sue."

Olivia was pleased too. She had heard plenty and seen photos, but it would be good to meet Jaz in the flesh.

"I'll show her what it means," he said. "Whether I'm in for the long haul or not, she needs to understand this has the potential to be a way of life."

Olivia raised an eyebrow.

"You never know," said Milo.

Jaz arrived an hour later – in a convoy of three cars. She had brought eight friends: three male, five female.

Olivia's first thought was how they might be useful while they were at the Vines. While the rules said they couldn't help with grape production, there were plenty of other jobs. Perhaps some weeding?

She needn't have troubled herself.

"This is a hoot!" Jaz declared.

"Where's the wine?" one her friends asked.

"Chambubbly for me," said another.

"I didn't know you were bringing the gang," said Milo.

Olivia detected a trace of annoyance in his voice. Jaz's look suggested this was normal. Maybe it was. Maybe Milo was the one at odds with his own kind.

The next thing Olivia knew, the gang was exiting out the back like a plague of locusts, running up among the vines and shouting. She just stood with Sue, staring and wondering what purpose these people had on the planet.

Then they turned and came roaring back.

"Pub!" someone yelled.

"We passed two on the way!" another declared.

And they were out the front door and away down the lane, leaving their cars. Jaz was the last of them.

"See you later," she called.

"What was that?" Sue eventually said.

"Oh, they don't mean any harm," said Milo. "They'll just have some lunch and probably do a review for Trip Advisor."

Milo and Sue went back inside, but Olivia stayed at the open door. She'd spotted Ken and Beano coming along.

"What was all that excitement?" he asked.

"Just visitors," said Olivia, swatting away a horsefly. "We'll soon send them away again."

It felt strange saying that, as if she were a local.

"Beano looks well," she said. "He got over that ailment then?"

"Yes, Milo paid for him to go to the vet."

"Did he? He never said."

Milo, you…

"All well out the back?" Ken asked.

"All's well, Ken. I'm just hell-bent on getting it right now. I can't wait to see some grapes."

"There's no rush," said Ken. "It's a way of life. It will happen when it happens."

Olivia watched him go. She felt unable, unwilling to keep up a dual life. She had to quit her job in London and put everything into wine. She had told Gerry she was committing to it. But now it was time to tell Prior Grove.

But a doubt crept back.

What if she decided grapes weren't for her. Would she get back into lobbying two, three years from now? Would she want to? Certainly, she would have lost clients and contacts. But wasn't she being silly? If the vineyard didn't work out, she could sell her share and do something different in London. Whatever something different might be.

Ken turned and came back.

"Just a thought," he said.

"Oh?"

"There's a place up the road planting eight thousand new vines on Monday."

"Eight thousand? Wow. That's a lot of work."

"Yes, they use a laser beam to get straight lines. None of this 'left a bit, right a bit' style of the old days."

"Do you know what grapes they chose?"

"Oh, you know me. I only pick up the odd bits and pieces. Pinots, I think. Gris, noir and Meunier. And some chardonnay, I think."

"Right."

"It's all matched to the soil, aspect and microclimate, of course. No point in leaving anything to chance."

"No indeed. Back-breaking work though."

"Not necessarily. Of course, they could always do with a hand."

"Oh?"

"None of my business, of course, but, you know, a helping hand is always welcome."

"Thing is, we've got really tight schedules, Ken."

"Absolutely. And that's how it should be. Besides, they've probably got enough hands, what with all those acres and that winery over there."

"They have a winery? That's still something we need to get signed up."

"I can't say I know much about it, really. Just that a helping hand or six might be useful. Bye for now."

She watched him toddle off. This easily overlooked old man was influencing the way she worked more and more.

"Ken? You didn't say the name of the place."

"It's Ramsey's," he called back without turning. "You've been there before, remember?"

Sunday morning saw Olivia up early. She took a shower that ran from hot to cold and then freezing. Then she dressed fast, had a quick bit of toast, and walked into the village to get a few extra bits, seeing as Milo and Sue would be staying over on Sunday night.

On her return, Milo decided to go out for a drive. He wanted to get a better sense of the surrounding countryside. Meanwhile, Leo arrived to do a job at Cam's. Apparently, Cam had restarted his renovation project in earnest. It seemed something had motivated him.

Sue went to help supervise but returned when it got cold and messy.

Two hours later, Leo finished his job for Cam and popped in to say hello. Olivia took the opportunity to report her cold shower moment.

Leo moved in close.

"If you need a shower, you can use my place. Fully tiled, fluffy towels, underfloor heating…"

It was a moment of romantic tension.

"That's very kind, Leo," said Sue, emerging from the kitchen. "Shall we draw up a schedule?"

"Actually, no need, Sue. Let me see if I can fix yours for you."

Sue shrugged and announced she was popping back to check on Cam.

"He's in his caravan," said Leo. "The side gate's open."

Sue left, leaving Leo and Olivia alone.

"So… a whole house to ourselves," said Leo.

Olivia couldn't decide what to do. She had a strong

urge to pick Leo up, haul him to her bed, throw him down and jump on him. But she hadn't finished with Gerry and that made it feel wrong. The urge for two people to throw themselves at each other was a strong one, but sometimes…

Leo took a step forward. Olivia took four. They kissed. Milo came in.

"Look what I've brought," he announced as they pulled apart.

It was a box of pastries.

"Oh, just the job," said Olivia.

Being denied Leo was just about offset by the lure of a raspberry Danish. Living and working on the land had seen her shed half a stone. The occasional pastry was no longer a worry. More a joy.

"Sue…"

She made them coffee and then sped off with a couple of pastries on a plate for Sue and Cam. After all, Sue was definitely partial to something sweet and tasty.

But as she neared…

That's odd.

The little caravan was rocking.

Ahh… I don't suppose they need pastries right now.

22

How To Plant 8,000 Vines in a Hurry

It was seven a.m. on a well-behaved Monday.

"Thanks for coming," said Jack Ramsey as they got out of Milo's car. "Every hand helps lighten the load."

They were soon walking into a large barren expanse that, as predicted by Ken the previous evening, had been spread with fertilizer and chalk, and been harrowed to mix it all in.

Olivia stifled a yawn and wondered what they had let themselves in for. Sue though seemed perky, as if walking on air.

"So, what's the plan?" asked Milo.

"First up, we plant our vines by machine. Have you seen that done before?"

"No," said Milo. Olivia and Sue shook their heads too.

"We've got a specialist team in," said Jack, "so we're the backup and follow-up team."

He took them over to the tractor with the vine-planting set-up hooked to the back. There they said hello to the planting crew.

"Basically, these two chaps sit on the machine and feed in the vines. The machine creates a furrow, see... then the spokes go round and lay in the vine... and then the machine closes the furrow behind it. That's one vine planted every few seconds."

"Amazing," said Milo. "Must be very cost-effective."

"It is," said Jack.

"We keep it nice and straight using GPS and laser guidance," said one of the planting crew.

Olivia almost felt this was too much technology for the countryside.

"It's very precise," said Jack. "We'll plant the first row straight down, then we'll have parallel rows with an eight-foot alley."

"Amazing," said Sue. "And I was thinking how it's a shame to lose the old ways."

"There's no room for sentiment in the fields, Sue," said Jack. "We run a business."

Olivia agreed. Despite the picture book attraction of the old ways, the countryside clearly had every right to embrace new technology. Anyone seeking to be a part of the life out here would be foolish to rely solely on tradition.

"So, when do we start?" she asked.

"We're just waiting for the butcher to open up," said Jack, in a way that made it sound obvious.

"Butcher?" said Sue.

Olivia almost felt like apologizing for her cousin's dim query over something country folk would find so obvious. She didn't though.

"Um," she said. "Sorry to be a bit thick, but butcher?"

"When we're planting, we have to buy the vines in advance. To keep them from becoming active before they're in the ground, we keep them cold, at around four to six degrees centigrade. Only, we don't have a cold store, but we know a man who does."

"The butcher?"

"Yes, Josh. He runs a butcher's shop in the village."

At around half-seven, Josh and co. arrived with the vines. Olivia had visions of huge bushes on the back of twenty flatbed trucks, but the vines were tiny, like bunches of pencils, albeit with hairy loose roots. They easily fitted into the vans that brought them.

The setting up of the machinery took a little while, which allowed something Gerry once said about vineyards to surface in her thoughts — and not for the first time.

"Jack, do you ever worry about bad years?"

Jack nodded slowly. "It's hard to completely ignore the possibility, but the way we look at it is this — if you're going to have a bad year, fine. Because, guess what, you're going to have bumper years too. And I'll tell you something, we've done alright over the years. More than alright. We wouldn't be investing in more vines and a bigger winery if we weren't."

Eventually, off to their right, the two men were seated on the planting machine, ready to feed the vines into the chain gear which would in turn feed them in behind each spoke going into the earth.

Jack's wife, Elsa came up from the house to greet the helpers. Her main concern was to follow a chart she'd prepared to ensure they didn't lose track of which vines were going where.

Studying it, Olivia couldn't help noticing the details relating to clones and rootstocks.

"It's important to know what each row gives us," Elsa explained. "Data is king for a vineyard. We want to know everything, from planting, to growth, to when buds break through, and in later years, the weight of the crop, acidity and sugar levels, and a load of other stuff that would bore non-vineyard people to death."

"I'm definitely not bored," said Olivia. "Fascinated, more like."

"Well, we're having the pinot gris in first, up on the western side. The wind comes up from the southwest mainly and that's a tougher grape to form a wind break for the pinot noir, which isn't so tough. Then we've got pinot Meunier in the final third."

"No chardonnay?" asked Olivia.

"Not this time, but we have plenty in the other field. This is actually to balance us up."

"To produce fizz?"

"To produce *more* fizz. A *lot* more. We like to provide a range, but fizz is where we're aiming to go big. Customers can't get enough of it. In fact, we only just bought this field off the Bradens last year for that very purpose. Are you looking to expand at your place?"

"Not just yet," said Milo. "We're still struggling to straighten out what we have."

The roar of a tractor engine tore through the air, cutting off the conversation. They were ready to go.

No sooner the planting machine reached the start of the first row, the men on the back began feeding the tiny, almost pathetic-looking vines into the wheel to be dropped at precise intervals into the shallow furrow that would close behind them, leaving just the tops of the vine poking up from the soil. Their pace along the field was much quicker than Olivia had imagined. It seemed almost too quick and she worried they might miss a few – but they hit home every time, vine after vine, in a laser-straight row.

Once the first row was completed, the tractor team reloaded. It was an impressive sight. Olivia could only imagine the months and years that Charlie and Gloria had taken to create their vineyard by the old-fashioned method.

With the tractor working on the next row, two teams followed to start putting in the first row's steel vine posts. Again, they didn't look as traditional as wooden posts, but Olivia guessed they would last a lot longer. Certainly, some of the wood at the Vines was looking past its best.

"It's the bit I feel odd about," said Elsa. "We make it look like a science experiment on Mars."

"I expect it'll soon blend in," said Sue.

"Oh definitely," said Elsa. "But first we have to set up the trellising and run miles and miles of wire. I half expect us to start digging trenches for a First World War battle."

Olivia had read up on it and understood. This is how you prepared. There was no attractive way to do it. You needed a wire to take the weight of the fruit and two double sets of movable wires for the canopy of leaf and canes that would make this a more familiar vineyard sight come the summer.

That aside, she was beginning to wonder if they had a role after all – at which, Elsa started handing out stacks of flat-packed vine guards. These had to be individually opened to form a square-edge tube to be placed over each vulnerable vine. The idea was to provide each plant with its own mini-greenhouse and rabbit guard.

As Sue fitted the first protective sheath over the first vine, she uttered, "one down, seven thousand, nine hundred and ninety-nine to go."

Now Olivia knew they were most definitely needed.

Several back-breaking hours later, the planting team was finished and Jack's mum, winery manager Kate, provided a lunch of hot pies, pastries, tea and coffee. The teams descended on it like locusts.

After lunch, the planting team departed to go to a smaller job twenty miles away, while Olivia, Sue and Milo gave another few hours' help – both with the vine guards and helping Jack and his team replace a few failing vines from the last planting.

The day ended at four. Olivia was exhausted and pleased in equal measure. She felt like having a giant group hug, but guessed this was a normal day for country folk.

"Group hug," said Elsa.

This was quickly followed by Jack's even more enticing call.

"To the winery!"

Kate welcomed them, although the first thing they shared was a tray of cold beers.

"Too dangerous to work off a day-long thirst with wine," said Kate.

Olivia was in full agreement.

"I have to drive," said Milo.

"I'll pay for a cab," said Elsa. "You can pick the car up tomorrow."

Milo smiled. He clearly wanted that beer.

Once their thirsts were quenched, they got stuck into the barbecue food that Jack's daughters arranged. Olivia was beginning to sense something shifting once again in her being. This wasn't London life. This was different.

Once everyone had eaten and relaxed, Kate, Jack and Elsa started the next event. Wine tasting.

"Now we have some very good fizz," said Kate, "but before we get to it I'd like you to try some wines in progress. First up, last year's crop, a lovely rosé base. This will eventually be bottled for fizz."

Olivia liked the look – bright and pink. And the taste. Fruity with a tang. Having read a hundred blogs and articles on wine, she knew how it would go through secondary fermentation in the bottle to create the bubbles.

"What do you think?" asked Elsa. "Would you blend it with something more complex from an oak barrel? And to what degree?"

"Interesting," said Sue.

Milo shook his head. "From what I've been reading on wine-making, you're asking someone who can't drive a go-kart to take a racing car for a spin."

Olivia nodded. "I wouldn't know where to start, Elsa."

"Well, that's the thing with winemaking," said Kate. "It's all about opinions based on experience. No-one can say for definite, but we can be reasonably sure of when to blend, how long to store on lees and if two or three years will pay off or not. That's why we have a nice man called Archie come over from Canterbury on a regular basis. He's our winemaker."

Two or three years...

Olivia wondered about the quality of wine they would produce from their own vines. Yes, they could give Jo a bottle of fizzy plonk to get the deeds, but beyond that? Would it be worth staying on at least until they had produced the best possible wine from this year's crop – even if that meant two or three years? It felt like a good challenge. No prizes, no penalties. Just the personal satisfaction of being able to say with pride "we made this."

It was a big commitment though.

Next, they tried a three-year old sparkling wine.

"This one is almost ready to go," said Kate. "Archie is looking to do a final tasting at the end of the year. Then we should be all-good for next year."

Olivia let the foaming wine settle in her glass. She sniffed and took a sip.

"Oh, very good," she said, almost laughing.

"Great balance," said Elsa.

All agreed that wine-making was an art all by itself, but one worth getting to know – after all, who could resist wine-tasting?

Once they were done, Jack directed them to a deep iced tray holding a dozen chilled bottles.

"And here we have something we're selling in our shop and at local supermarkets… for you to enjoy on us."

A cheer went up and glasses were quickly filled. And when Jack and Elsa's daughters put some music on, Olivia felt the winery setting was as good as any pub she'd ever been in.

"Have you thought about which winery you'll use?" Jack asked. "I know you were up here a while back, but…"

"Well, we were hoping…" said Olivia, hoping he might offer.

"We have the capacity," said Elsa. "And we can always do a good deal for friends."

Olivia felt a surge of emotion. This had been a perfect day. And all down to an elderly man who, in London, she would have passed by on the street without a word between them.

"Thank you, Ken," she whispered.

Whatever had happened last year regarding a winery, this year they would be dealing with Ramsey's. She would email Jo the solicitor in the morning and advise her where to send the money Gloria had set aside for this year's production.

Around eight, returning to the Vines in a cab, Olivia took in the passing countryside. This was the picture postcard view, steeped in long shadows from the sinking sun and lovely it was too. But Olivia was beginning to understand the other countryside. A place of working and living, of tradition and change. It looked sleepy, but it was alive.

She felt a connection.

Or maybe the sparkling wine had buoyed her into a reverie.

Or perhaps it was thoughts of Leo.

The fields, the hills, the streams, the hedgerows flashed by the window… and reminded her of a train journey down from London, wondering about the impending reading of a will. Only, now she felt part of something.

23

Decisions, Decisions

Gerry texted. He had the figures. To Olivia it was like a bad smell. After the fresh air and fresh hope of their vine-planting at Ramsey's, Gerry seemed stale and burdensome.

He had the figures...

It was a Tuesday, just before lunchtime at Prior Grove. Milo was doing his stint at the Vines, which meant Sue would be in a school office living what would appear to be a normal life.

Olivia texted Sue the details. She'd wait for her elder cousin's advice and then put it to Milo.

Sue came straight back.

'Don't trust him.'

They agreed to wait until lunchtime and then get on the phone.

Despite the time seeming to drag on forever, Olivia was eventually walking up Buckingham Gate to the Palace with her phone pressed to her ear.

"I don't want to be sucked into Gerry's vortex without

anyone knowing."

"He's poison, Olivia. Run away before he bullies you into something you'll regret."

"I know what you mean, but I've never run away from responsibility. He's been good for me in the past. That might have ended now but he deserves to be let down gently."

"I don't trust him, Olivia. I really don't."

"Alistair dropped me like a stone. It's not nice."

"Have you told Milo yet?"

"No, but I will."

"Well, make sure he sees the figures."

"I will."

"And don't sign anything."

"I won't. I'm seeing Gerry tomorrow after work. I'll let you know how it goes."

"Well, okay, but be brave and be firm. Don't let him push you around."

"I won't."

"And be careful."

Olivia returned to the office feeling awkward. Not so long ago, she had wanted to live with him. Now she had to tell him it was over – face to face.

The following day after work, Olivia took the Tube up to Northwood Station, where Gerry picked her up. He said they'd go to a local pasta and pizza place. Except, when they arrived, they didn't get out of the car.

"I thought we could talk in private before we eat," he said. "I take it you've gone over the figures. I've got a client lined up waiting to spend big money. I'm giving the whole thing over to you. All you have to do is manage the situation. It's the easiest thing you'll ever do."

"Thanks Gerry, but I've made up my mind about what I'm going to do."

"I haven't finished yet. I'm also putting you on the board of two of my other companies. All I need is thirty-five grand. You need to get Milo excited about it. He'll make a killing."

"I'm not selling my share to Milo. Especially not for thirty-five thousand. We'll have the deeds around New Year."

"You're not listening. I'm going to put a hundred grand in your account long before then. Eighteen months from now, you'll be holding two hundred grand, maybe more. You'll be way ahead of Milo. Plus, he might not get half what he thinks at an auction."

"Let's eat, Gerry. It's been a long day and I'm hungry."

At the restaurant, they ate in the most unrelaxed manner. For Olivia, it was the opposite of being a pleasure and she put away her mushroom pizza far too quickly.

When they emerged into the evening air, she decided it was time.

"If you could drive me back to the station, Gerry, that would be great."

Gerry drove them to the station and beyond.

"Gerry?"

"There's a quiet little spot five minutes from here."

"I don't really feel up to it. Indigestion."

Gerry said nothing. Five minutes later, they were still driving.

Sue texted. 'I investigated Gerry.'

What?

"Who's that?" Gerry asked. "Milo?"

"No, it's a work thing," Olivia lied.

She read on. 'He isn't living at his house. He's in a

cheap bed and breakfast place in Watford. I spoke to his wife. They divorced eight months ago. He's bust.'

Olivia typed a response.

'You only have his wife's word for that.'

Sue replied.

'Milo checked. He's a registered bankrupt.'

A few minutes later, they pulled into a quiet lane alongside a heathland.

"I do love you," said Gerry. "I probably should say it more often."

"I'm not sure this is helping us, Gerry."

"I want to take you away. Somewhere nice. Somewhere hot. There are other things I want too."

Olivia realized he was chewing a mint – just the thing for her indigestion.

"Gerry, do you have—"

"Just give me a minute."

He was out of the car and heading for some bushes for a pee. Olivia's indigestion rose up.

Mints…

She checked her bag but was out of the flippin' things. Without a thought, she checked the glove compartment. No mints. Just hire car stuff.

Oh shit, this isn't his car.

Olivia felt any remaining control of the situation slipping away. This wasn't so much shaky ground as a landslide. Gerry was a liar. He wanted her money to… to what? It didn't matter. There were no companies, no opportunities. She felt physically sick.

Then she got out.

Gerry was returning.

"I need to go home," she said. "We're finished."

He came over and grabbed her arm.

"We're not finished, Liv. We're just getting started.

There's a bright future out there waiting for us."

"I know everything."

"How do you mean."

"A friend of mine spoke to your wife."

"You've been spying on me?"

"Could you let go of my arm, please?"

"Who was it? Sue or Milo?"

"It doesn't matter."

"Don't tell me – they checked and found I went bust. Is that it? I can explain everything."

"I don't care that you lied to me. That's you hitting rock bottom, not me. I've found a new life for myself. I don't even know if it's going to work out, but I feel right in trying."

Gerry squeezed her arm tighter.

"You're hurting me, Gerry."

"No, it's you doing the hurting. At least you're trying to – but you won't hurt me because I'm strong. You? You're pathetic. Pissing around on that pile of dung. You know nothing about wine, nothing about business. You could have helped me get back on my feet, but no, you had to kick me. No matter. I'll live. As for you though…"

Olivia started trembling.

"Please don't do anything silly."

He squeezed her arm to the bone, making her squeal.

"You think I was going to marry you? I was just using you for fun. It was only the thought you might have some money coming that kept me interested. You're a boring, lame, unsexy lightweight who's faking it in the countryside. You're pathetic."

He thrust her sideways so hard, her legs couldn't make sense of the trajectory. She hit the ground, jarring a number of bones.

Looking up, she watched Gerry get in the car and rev

the engine. Then he turned in a tight circle, too close for comfort, and roared away into the night.

It was over. Not how she'd planned it. But it was over. Sitting in a puddle, in the dark, somewhere northwest of London, her new life could begin.

She phoned Sue.

"Olivia?"

"He's gone, Sue. It's over."

"Are you okay?"

"He hurt my arm. I don't think it's broken…"

"Ooh, what an absolute… bastard! Now, where are you?"

"I don't know. Hang on, I'll go on the maps thing and get my location."

It turned out Sue was only a twenty-minute drive away, so while Olivia had to suffer a painful ten-minute walk back to civilization, she was soon in a cab to Sue's place in North Harrow.

Sue was brilliant. A total fuss-maker. They worked out that Olivia had suffered heavy bruising but nothing worse and that her clothes needed a wash. Then it was decided by rule of Dictator Sue that Olivia would have the bed, and Sue the couch.

Olivia's head hit the pillow that night in a state of varied emotions. She was happy to have family like Sue and Milo, relieved to be rid of Gerry, bruised from being told she was a fake and a lightweight, and apprehensive about her next step. You didn't just walk out on a job in London after ten years.

Except sometimes you had to.

*

The following day, the Tube journey to work seemed strange. Yes, it was another line from another part of London, but the strangeness was its sameness – too many people trying to squeeze inside the train, too many miserable-looking so-and-so's infecting other passengers with their gloom…

The guy next to Olivia was happy though. He was playing some daft game on his phone with the sound bleeding through his ear pods. What was he? A lawyer? A civil servant? A good degree from a top university, no doubt – and yet he was trying to fight little red blobs to an annoying diddly-diddly tune.

More people got on, increasing the level of stuffiness and sweatiness. Olivia felt sure she hadn't breathed any oxygen for at least two stops. Then a seated woman suddenly bobbed up and made for the doors. With the speed of an Olympic athlete, Olivia was thumping her rear onto the vacated seat.

Relieved, she retrieved her earpieces from her bag, plugged in to Adele and flicked through the free newspaper.

On page five there was an earth-shattering shock. 'Celebrities Who Battle Cellulite' was the headline. Olivia was aghast. Forget foreign wars and terrorist plots; there were half a dozen marginally-famous people with cellulite. Why wasn't the U.N. setting up an international response team? What was the White House doing? Had the matter even been discussed in Parliament? Olivia could only hope those clever scientists in all those hi-tech labs were quitting medical research to sort this problem out.

A while later, at work, sipping hot tea at her desk, she took to blinking her eyes for extended periods. As much as she had loved being at Sue's it was difficult to sleep with so much going on in her head. Now her body was attempting to make up for it. Of course, it wasn't technically sleeping at your desk if you were merely blinking – and who decided what constituted a blink? Surely they could last five or ten seconds?

Oops, that one felt like twenty seconds...

She opened her eyes. Henry was staring at her from his glass fishbowl office.

Olivia busied herself with a new project. The client was something to do with a proposed new road.

Later, returning from a pre-lunch trip to the ladies' room, Henry stopped her to introduce Trudy, a new boss. As far as Olivia could tell, she was a female version of Henry, brought across from the partner company.

"This is Olivia," Henry said. "One of our most trusted and valuable employees. We've cherished and nurtured Olivia for many years now. She knows the ropes, so no need to worry about what you say, Trudy."

Olivia smiled. She didn't need to put up with this semi-legal outfit anymore.

"If you need me, Trudy, I work in the corner by the emergency exit."

Somewhat perplexed, Trudy gazed at Olivia and then stared out toward her corner.

"Do you? It's certainly—"

"—a long way off? Yes, it is. Perhaps Henry could lend you his binoculars."

"Thank you, Olivia," Henry said, dismissing her.

"Yes, thank you," said Trudy.

"No problem," said Olivia. "If the building catches fire, you can say hi as you make your way out."

Back at her desk, she kept an eye on Henry and waited. He'd be over as soon as Trudy was out of the way. Of course, that meant listening to Zara. Olivia tried to ignore her slurping her way through a microwaved pot of noodles, but Zara's tongue and lips were making a noise like a farting hippopotamus.

Sluuuuuuuuuuuuuuuuuuuuuuuuuuuurrrrrp...

Olivia shuddered.

Sluuuuuuuuuuuuuuuuuuuuuuuuuuuurrrrrp...

Olivia started humming "Food, Glorious Food" to herself.

Sluuuuuuuuuuuuuuuuuuuuuuuuuuuurrrrrp...

Two minutes later, it was over.

Thank God.

But... Zara got started on a pot of lite raspberry rice.

How can you eat out of so many fricking pots?

Clink.

Olivia was furious. Why did Zara have to clink and clunk the stupid spoon against her stupid teeth?

Clink. Clunk.

Arghhh.

Resisting the urge to grab the spoon and shatter all Zara's teeth, Olivia checked her phone for news of something, anything.

Laura came over to hand something to Zara.

Laura...

She had replaced Cass.

And Henry... he had replaced old Dan who retired.

Dan... completely forgotten no sooner he'd set foot out the door. Not a mention. Forgotten history. Reduced to nothing.

Olivia paid a quick visit to the store cupboard for a sheet of card. Once she had tri-folded it to make a desk placard, she wrote something on it with great care and purpose.

Then she grabbed her things and walked out. By the time any office discussion got under way, she would be long gone.

Of course, Henry and co. could say what they liked about the sign on her desk that stated quite simply:

'Olivia Holmes Has Inherited A Vineyard'.

24

Moving On

It was a sunny Saturday in New Cross and Olivia was packing her final bags of clothes into the car. It felt good. She had stopped short of putting her apartment up for sale – letting it instead to an American couple who would be in London for six months.

She had skipped working her one month's notice at Prior Grove on account of them sharing her duties between Rob, Zara, Laura and Carla. She hadn't been replaced by a whole person. Her desk had simply been removed and her role expunged. No one would ever be able to point and say Olivia Holmes sat there and did that job.

Before leaving New Cross, she stopped to get some bits in Sainsbury's. Although she was now a staunch supporter of the local shops in Maybrook, this was one occasion where she just wanted to get to the Vines and sort a few things out.

On the way back to her car with a half full trolley, she felt a mix of excitement and exhaustion. Everything was coming together now and it was proving an emotional drain.

"Liv?"

It was Alistair getting out of a new Honda.

"How's it going?" he asked.

His girlfriend was exiting the other side.

"Hello Liv," she called across the car's sunroof. It was only when she came around to join Alistair that Olivia could see the huge baby bump.

"Yes, good news, eh?" said Alistair.

Olivia still hadn't spoken, and was finding it hard to put her feelings into words.

"The timing was just kind of right," he continued. "I never wanted to be a dad, and then… I did. Hard to explain really. We're just really happy, aren't we, Steph?"

"Yes, we are, Stair."

Stair?

Since when did he have such a stupid pet name?

Olivia's brain was firmly in overload territory now. In twenty years, the timing had never been right. And in all that time, she had been calling him Alistair instead of Stair. How come she hadn't discovered the secret to his paternal side?

"So? All well?" Stair asked.

The first thing Olivia threw was a pizza. Not very damage-inflicting but she had to get that out of the way to get to the loose lemons and limes.

"Oww, that hurt. Stop it now, Liv. Liv! Oww."

He ran and hid behind the children's play rides, but she was now armed with eggs and a bag of flour. He would have got a side order of sour cream too had a security guard not wrestled her to the ground.

*

The delayed drive down to Kent was not a happy one. All she could think of was how it could be the right time. It wasn't fair. All those thousands of times they'd made love – now it seemed so pointless-pointless-pointless. She had wanted to become a mother and he'd stopped her. She should have gone on bloody strike. All that pleasure meant nothing now. Nothing at all. She'd been robbed. He ought to get time in jail.

Off the main road, the country lanes offered up their usual narrow runs and tight bends. One such bend also offered a ditch, which she drove into while imagining stuffing cream cakes into Alistair's face.

All went quiet.

Crap...

Then all the anger exploded out of her.

"Now look what you've made me do, Stair, you... you... fucking arse!"

She got out of the car. The ditch wasn't too deep and the damage not too great. She waited five minutes and then a Land Rover came along. The woman driving it – Wendy from Wrotham who had a cat called Dexter – used her vehicle's hook and pulley attachment to haul Olivia's car out of the ditch.

"I'd get it looked at," Wendy advised.

Olivia reached the Vines in one piece but not in a happy state of mind. For one thing, she had no eggs or flour to bake her celebratory 'moving in' cake.

"I'm back, Gloria. I won't live here as a reflection of you though. We'll be doing things my way."

This house with no history and no paintings of its past owners would have a fresh start. Milo had already texted with news that he could source cut-price bathroom tiles if

Sue and Olivia didn't mind duck egg blue. Then Sue called from over the fence. She and Cam would be getting a takeaway Chinese meal later. Did Olivia fancy joining them?

Up in the bedroom, placing some clothes in the wardrobe, she wondered about her great aunt.

"So, Gloria, did you ever have wild parties here? All night drinking? Come on, I'm going to find out sooner or later."

Once she had settled in, she decided to walk into the village. It would feel different this time. She'd be strolling to the shops to buy flour and eggs as a genuine local.

Up on the road by the bend, with her car in mind, she crossed to call in on Gus. He was in the little office taking payment from a fuel customer. He smiled when he saw her.

"I'm official now," she said as the customer departed. "I've moved in full-time."

"Good for you. What about money?"

Grrr, trust Gus to spoil the moment.

"I'll be fine. Unless you're offering me a nice little part-time job? I'll say yes."

"Thanks but no thanks. I'm overstaffed with just me."

"Well, okay – I actually called in to ask you about my car. I had a little accident. I think it's alright, but could you take a look for me?"

"Sure, just bring it over when you're ready."

"No appointment necessary?"

"Not for you."

In the High Street, Olivia decided to postpone buying any bits and pieces until after a pub lunch in the Royal Standard.

Annie the landlady was pleased for her, but worried about her money situation now that she'd packed in a job *with regular pay.*

What was it with country people and money?

Tucking into her cheese ploughman's at the bar, she switched to the Vines.

"One thing that bugs me, Annie, is the lack of photos. There is literally nothing. I mean I have no idea what Gloria looked like in her younger days and no idea of Charlie at all."

"Well, I don't know much about that," said Annie. "They lived there a fair while, but I can't recall them going to any weddings or New Year parties – you know, where people would be clicking away."

"They moved there in 1962. Do you know where they were before that?"

"They were definitely local. I'm not sure where they lived though."

She wondered if to ask Ken for details but felt he would be protective of Gloria's memory. Perhaps the Vines wasn't like Buckingham Palace or Raglington Hall. Perhaps its ghosts didn't want their pictures adorning the walls. Maybe the house itself preferred to stay anonymous.

Out in the vineyard, Olivia checked vine after vine. There was no doubt about it. The good weather had brought everything forward.

Ken didn't come by, so Olivia went to see him. He was wrapped in a blanket on the sofa and said he'd been laid up with a cold, but he didn't seem to be suffering from one. He looked more worn out than anything.

"Would you like me to call a doctor?" she asked.

Ken shook his head vigorously, so she settled for making him a hot lemon drink.

"I've moved in full-time, by the way," she called from the kitchen. "Do you think Gloria will mind?"

"I'm sure she won't," he called back.

She brought the drink in and made sure Ken was comfortable. While he sipped it, she studied the photos on his mantelpiece.

"That's my parents," he said of the one she was looking at. "Their wedding day back in the twenties."

The man and woman were dressed for the occasion, but something suggested they were poor people. Their complexions were sallow, their clothes not quite fitting.

"Were they local people?"

"No, East End of London."

"Really?"

"I was an evacuee during the War. They sent most kids out of London because of the bombs."

"Wow, so you were sent down here…"

"No, I was sent to Buckinghamshire, but I didn't get on with the people, so I ran away."

"To Kent? That's a long way."

"No, well, I ran away back to London, but there was a bombing raid…"

"Your parents?"

"No, thankfully, but my mum's family were wiped out. That's where I'd gone – to my grandparents. My dad would have killed me if I'd come home, see."

"You survived a bomb dropping on you?"

"I was the only one. So… well… this was the only other place I knew. Before the War, we used to come down to Kent in the summer to pick hops for beer. Everyone did. It was the only way families could get a break from the grime. Anyway, I sneaked onto a train at London Bridge and got off a few miles up the road from here."

"And you've been here ever since?"

"Well, no, I had to do two years in the army – National Service – and then I came back. Well, my girl was here, wasn't she."

"Gloria?"

"Yes, Gloria."

"Oh Ken. That's seems romantic and sad at the same time."

"We were teenagers at the end of the War. We said we'd always be together. Then I had to go into the army at eighteen. Anyway, she thought I'd been killed in Palestine, you know, when Israel was being founded, 1948, it was. I was on a train... I had a bomb blast injury and then came down with blood poisoning. Word got back to Kent via family in London who wanted me back with them."

"Your parents?"

"My mum. She told Gloria's parents I was dead."

"Oh my God."

"I was out of it for months. Then when I got back... well, she and Charlie were married."

"Oh Ken... that's appalling."

"Love of my life, she was."

"And you never got to be with her."

"Apart from a couple of times, no."

"What?"

"Well, there was the time before I went into the army, obviously, and then in 1962 when they bought the house and I was helping them move in – only Charlie was busy doing a bit of business elsewhere."

"Ken, I'm shocked. You old rascal."

"It wasn't anything like loose morals. We just looked at each and there was just too much love there. It just poured out of us. We couldn't help it. Afterward, we said we'd keep apart, of course. I mean we were decent people."

"I know that, Ken."

Olivia looked at another photo. It was Ken in uniform. He looked so young... so strong and handsome.

"Where does the time go, eh?" he asked.

She had no answer for him.

"Away from the past," she said, "we've had a real burst of activity with shoots."

"Oh right, sounds like it's time for a spot of bud-rubbing then. You want to get rid of any unwanted shoots off the trunk. And make sure you thin out any crowded shoots at the vine-head. That's the way to get good quality."

Olivia nodded. She'd already checked in with Viv and understood how extra shoots would suck nutrients and deprive the grapes.

She smiled. Wait until she told Cass she was going to spend time bud-rubbing.

Back at the Vines, sitting in Gloria's chair, Olivia pondered the bare mantelpiece. No photos. No memories, happy or sad.

She rose to look out over the garden.

Ken and Gloria...

Sometimes, first love goes so deep the memories of it hurt. She recalled her own. A boy from school. Keith. She could still feel the heat of her tears at their parting.

There was a knock at the door. It was Leo. She thought of Ken and Gloria's torrent of love and lust in this very house in 1962.

"I heard you've moved in for good," he said, grinning boyishly.

"News travels fast."

"You must come up to Bluebell Wood."

"Must I?"

"It's in full flower."

She was a local now. Why not?

She let Leo drive her two miles up the road. The wood was just off a narrow lane that reminded her of the orienteering challenge on the last Prior Grove team-building weekend. What challenges might lay ahead here, she wondered.

The carpet of bluebells was stunning. It swept through the forest floor between the trees and seemed to go on forever.

"They go mad, they do. They give everything to get their moment in the sun before the trees come into leaf. The forest floor gets dark then."

"Carp diem," said Olivia. "Seize the day."

"Exactly," said Leo.

She knew they were going to have an encounter. She just hoped it was the right thing to do, because she wanted it as much as he clearly did. With Leo in her life, and the Vines too, she would blend in with countryside living. She would be a country girl.

"Have you always lived in the area?" she asked.

"I grew up near Dover but my parents divorced when I was ten. I came here with my dad. Been here ever since."

"You've never settled down with anyone?"

"One time I did. We were together five years, but she wanted a family and I didn't. Maybe my parents fighting all those years put me off. Anyway, that's all ancient history now."

"Some people find it easy. They meet someone, fall in love, get a mortgage, have kids, don't have fights and carry on loving and living. My friend Cass is like that."

"Imagine all that happiness and fulfilment," said Leo. "It sounds like fake news to me. Are you sure they don't fight like wildcats when you're not there?"

"I'm sure they don't."

"Lucky Cass then."

"Yes."

"Yes... what a good word. Say it again and anything could happen."

"Really?" Olivia felt her temperature rising.

"You can whisper it in my ear, if you like. Or you could send me a text. Just say 'Yes', and you know the rest."

She laughed.

"I can't hear you," he said.

Olivia picked up a sturdy twig and found a patch of dirt. She wrote. Y...

She didn't get a chance to add the other letters, because Leo was pulling her gently to the ground between the trees, where they began to make love in the way she deserved. In a way that would create not just fireworks, but earthquakes.

25

Something in the Air

On a chilly Friday morning in mid-May, Olivia was out among the vines with Ken and Beano. It was an important moment. The small button-like flower clusters appearing on the shoots meant they had cleared another hurdle.

"I do like to see flowering," said Ken.

"Er, Ken, you seem to be looking at me, not the vines."

"Frost. That's your only worry."

"In mid-May?"

"Yes, May can have its moments. Once you've got advanced growth, you're at the mercy of a cold snap."

"To be fair, the forecast wasn't great."

"A hard, late frost is nuclear war, Olivia. Total obliteration. There's nothing you can do. Well, you could watch every TV weather bulletin for the next week. It'll make you ill with worry though. Probably best to pray."

Olivia nodded. "Don't worry. I won't become a weather worrier."

She spent the afternoon and early evening watching every weather bulletin, checking six weather sites on her phone and tuning in to the radio.

On TV, the weather presenter advised gardeners in the east and southeast to be aware of a potential late frost.

Gardeners? What about vineyard owners and farmers?

It was strange how she had watched thousands of weather bulletins wondering if it would be wet or dry, warm or chilly. Now it meant something more. A chance of a late frost in the southeast? It sounded more ominous than a turn of events in a Shakespearean tragedy.

That evening, Olivia decided to take the plunge and go to the pub by herself. Hopefully, she would see a familiar face or two. If not, she'd have a quick gin and tonic and flee back into the night.

As it was, her entrance at the Royal Standard was met warmly by Gus from the petrol station, who had fixed her car for a rock-bottom price. Not that she could go over and have a drink with him, as he also happened to be Gus the violinist in Folkie-Karaoke. Along with Harpo on the accordion and Killy on the acoustic guitar, they had a screen ready with the words of a hundred popular songs. You just got up and sang. It didn't matter if it was a rock song, or a soul ballad. Folkie-Karaoke would turn it into a folk classic.

It took two gin and tonics to work up enough courage, and then landlady Annie's suggestion of going for "Take Me Home Country Roads" seemed a good idea and bad idea rolled into one.

She sang it though and needn't have worried. Most of the twenty other people in the bar sang it with her.

Later, she walked back from the pub alone and aware

of the chill in the air. It was cold. Too damned cold.

Back at home, she checked her phone as she settled into bed. There was still that chance. She felt like getting out of bed again and going outside. It didn't matter if she froze to death – not when her duvet might provide protection for one of the vines.

She stirred again at two a.m. and got up to look out of the window. Half-expecting to find the countryside covered in thick snow, she was relieved to see just a damp vista in the moonlight.

The following morning, she hurried outside. All was well and the sun was rising into a blue sky. However, the smug simpleton giving the TV weather forecast said the threat of frost would continue. So, another sleepless night filled with fear and dread awaited her. Country life was losing its sparkle. It was too fraught with unseen danger.

She spent the day plucking out weeds, but it was all done in the knowledge that she might be wasting her time.

When she saw Ken, he mentioned plant nutrition. But Olivia couldn't concentrate on the words coming out of his mouth.

After lunch, she checked her phone. The weather report suggested there was no longer a likelihood of frost.

What? When had this life-affecting change taken place? Why wasn't there a special report on the TV news? She even phoned the Meteorological Office to confirm it.

There would be no frost! She laughed. And then she felt tears pricking her eyes.

"Is there anything else I can help you with?" asked the Met Office person on the other end of the line.

*

Two and a half weeks later, out among the vines in hot weather, Olivia, Sue and Milo were happy with the progress of the flowering process. The micro-clusters had grown to the point where they could make out the individual flowers.

"I reckon we're almost ready for fertilization," said Milo.

Olivia nodded. They had been waiting for this – the more advanced stage of flowering when pollination and fertilization would take place.

"Keep calm though, Sue," said Milo, "it won't be a saucy sex show."

"Thank you, Milo, but I'm well aware of how vines are fertilized."

"Seems a shame though," said Milo, "having to self-fertilize. I mean they're missing out on all that fun with another plant. Imagine doing it yourself. It must be like those times we humans—"

"Milo, this is the countryside, not a comedy club."

Olivia liked having Sue and Milo come down together. Despite the occasional teasing, she felt that Milo had found a much-needed older friend in Sue. And, even though she occasionally blushed, Olivia felt Sue was getting a lot out of it too.

"Dry weather with a slight breeze," said Milo. "Perfect for picnics, outdoor naughtiness and vine pollination. What do you reckon, Liv?"

Olivia reckoned all three sounded good but changed the subject.

"Vineyard Viv says she loves bees getting involved in pollination, but admits it's just a soft, romantic notion."

All three had done their homework on self-pollinating vines, of course, and knew the caps on the buds would come off, pollen would be dropped, and the breeze would dust it over the waiting stamens. The result would be tiny, healthy, bouncing, baby grape berries, unless, as Viv said quite darkly, "one the things that *can* go wrong *does* go wrong."

Fortunately, she had a special dance to ward off evil anti-fertility spirits.

Olivia loved Viv's upbeat outlook on grape growing and life in general. Who was she? Did she have a life story? Or could people live in video blogs and not actually exist outside of that? She hoped Viv was having a good day and put a comment on YouTube thanking her.

Leo texted.

'I'm outside. Any chance of tea or coffee?'

Olivia went to let him in. He kissed her no sooner the door was closed, but she warned him of Milo and Sue being out the back.

"Liv, you mean you're worried they might catch us having coffee?"

She took him out to say hello to her cousins. Leo was easy going and affable. He was also a country boy and nodded his appreciation at progress in the vineyard.

"I've said it before and I'll say it again. You're doing a great job, guys."

Olivia wanted him, but it would have to wait.

The following day, with Milo and Sue back in London, the weather changed. A colder, wetter front came up from the southwest. Gusts of wind were strong enough to cause a rustle.

"Stay back, wind!" Olivia ordered.

She had read enough to know that too much wind and certainly heavy rain could cause havoc. The thought of having most of their flowers remaining unfertilized and unable to produce grapes... it was too scary to contemplate. Good pollination was essential for a good fruit set and a successful harvest.

The rain came. Heavy and hard.

It didn't last though. The sun came out again and Nature continued to go about its business. In truth, the vines were advancing nicely, the flowers were blooming, and Viv was saying it was a good time to start planning the harvest. This mainly seemed to involve building a list of helpers well in advance of the event. Olivia felt the length of time needed was probably so they could arrange blackmail and bribery on a suitably grand scale.

Out on the land away from the vineyard, Olivia had taken to walking up the lane and into the fields across the road. There was a lovely public footpath that took in a number of glorious views. She thought back to last November and the view of a Victorian folly. It seemed like something to look at. This felt like something to belong to. Wildflowers were everywhere, in every hue. She took photos so that she could look them up at her leisure. Why? Because she wanted to know. And that told her how much this place was coming to mean to her.

Back at the Vines, Ken suggested thinking about picking off the smallest bunches after fruit-setting. He said this would improve the quality of the grapes they kept. It sounded like a good idea. It wouldn't affect their yield too much but they would have higher quality grapes.

Olivia was learning more and more. It was becoming a something far greater than an interest. Checking over the pinot Meunier's flour-dusted leaf undersides, everything looked so good.

"I know who you are," she told the vine. "Dusty Miller."

She had learned that Meunier was French for miller and that their pinot Meunier vines would produce a grape with black skin and white juice.

"I know all your secrets. I seriously don't know why you hang around with chardonnay and pinot noir. You do all that hard work helping them make up the blend for champagne then your name gets left off the label. I'd complain if I were you. But don't worry; we'll mention you on our label."

The pinot gris was looking good too. That would make a lovely pinot grigio wine. All these healthy plants, despite the violence they had received in the jaws of six sets of secateurs back in winter.

Leo stopped by. Olivia showed him the progress among the vines.

"They'll soon be full of grapes," he said. "I'll be able to take a grape... feel it's softness when I press gently... and if I press a little more, its juice will dribble out... for me to taste."

Olivia led him straight up to Gloria's old room where they made love. At one point, a flash of Gloria raced through Olivia's mind, but she was only a fleeting ghost.

At the end of June, the air was very warm – perfect for buying cheap emulsion to freshen up the main bedroom, lounge and hall. Although the real refurbishment would have to wait, there was no need for drab rooms when a temporary fix of a hundred quid's worth of paint, plus a couple of rugs donated by Sue, could give the place a lift.

Olivia had also been to see how Jack and Elsa Ramsey were getting on. The dry weather was no good for their newly planted vines, but their daughters enjoyed the excuse to haul a water bowser behind a quadbike to get the job done.

However, Kate Ramsey warned that continuing dry weather would challenge even the established vines and that they should all consider performing a rain dance. Olivia was the only one to laugh – but she stopped short when she realized they were serious.

Back at the Vines, she checked Vineyard Viv for guidance, and then did what she assumed to be an actual rain dance. It looked like a glimpse of the world's worst nightclub. It didn't bring rain either.

Later, Ken came to look.

"Hmm, tendrils browning. I expect the sap's showing too much calcium. Have you tried doing a rain dance?"

"It didn't work."

"Maybe two of us will have more luck."

"What?"

"Double the power."

"You can't be serious?"

"These are your vines we're talking about."

And so Olivia and Ken did a rain dance together.

And she recalled her dad in the rain. Coming to collect her from an after-school club. Tomorrow would be the 30th anniversary of him taking his own life. And so, this one time only, his spirit joined them in their dance.

That evening, Leo came over for dinner. And stayed late. In the bedroom, entwined as one, Olivia felt more empowered than ever. She was truly merging with country life.

"Maybe we should take this to the next level," she said, while resting in his arms as her breathing and heart rate returned to normal.

"How do you mean? I'm worn out from this level."

"I feel like I've switched worlds... like my old life has gone for good. I feel I'm part of this world now. I want us to be together."

"We are together."

"I mean live together."

Leo sat up.

"I'm not into that kind of thing, Liv. This is great as it is. Don't you think?"

She looked up at him. Her heart rate was going back up again.

"I'm not selling my share in the Vines. I'm not leaving. I'm staying."

"I'm not into commitment, Liv. I thought we were good as we are. It's fun, right?"

"Fun isn't enough to make a relationship last, Leo."

Even as she said it she knew she'd spoken for him.

"I thought, as a London type..."

"I'm not a London type. I'm not any type. I'm me."

Leo got up and started dressing.

"I'm not into relationships, Liv. I find them stifling. Why can't you just see this for what it is?"

Olivia sat up in bed.

"I thought this was the start of something."

"No, this is the whole thing."

"You don't have to go."

"Oh, I do. Before those hooks sink in deep. I'm not your man, Liv. I'm not into relationships."

She watched him finish dressing and leave the room without looking back... and she listened to him closing the front door behind him.

To the sound of his van driving off, she settled back into bed and stared up at the ceiling.

"I suppose you think it's funny?"

But Gloria didn't answer.

"Do I really look like some shallow, city type coming down to the country to have fun? I thought I had a bit more depth than that."

Evidence of Leo having been in her bed remained – his aftershave, his sweat, his essence. All that would have to go. In fact, she'd change the sheets and take a shower right away. Then, when she woke up in the morning, there would be no reminder of her wrong turn in life.

"Gloria? That heart-opening thing? It's over. Closed and bolted shut."

Later, in bed, between fresh sheets, there was a pitter-patter on the roof. It dragged Olivia's mood out of the doldrums. She even grudgingly smiled at Nature's work.

Then the heavens opened.

Olivia went downstairs and stood by the open back door until the storm passed. Then she ran out with a torch.

Following fruit set, the grape berries were green and hard to the touch. They had very little sugar and were high in organic acids. But they would soon reach half their final size and the stage of veraison – the beginning of the ripening process.

"Stay with me, guys," she yelled across the acres.

She returned to her bed, tired and happy with the countryside.

"I'm still learning," she told Gloria, although whether that referred to vines or people was lost to sleep.

26

Echoes

It was early July and the weather was hot. A succession of days reached into the high twenties, or as Ken preferred, around the eighties. Whichever measurement, these were warm days with barely a breeze. Still air, silent except for the hum of a bee, the twitter of a small bird…

Olivia tried not to concern herself with the downpours they'd had – especially around pollination. Trusting and praying was all they could do. Everything was in flower to varying degrees. This was country life. You couldn't hurry Mother Nature. There was no app for that. It was hot and dry so you just had to get water to the vines – by hose and by canister on a wheelbarrow.

Jobwise, apart from extensive watering, the next thing on the agenda was to begin the process of tucking up – another phrase Cass would have fun with. She'd have to remind her to come down. She'd love the place.

Out in the vineyard, tucking up was easy work made hard by long hours and the raging sun. A straw hat was just the thing.

According to Vineyard Viv, the tucking up itself was simply arranging individual canes to be contained within the trellis wires. But the hot weather had made the canes brittle, so it was slower work than hoped for. Olivia understood. This was production. The countryside looked picturesque in summer, but it was a giant outdoor factory.

So it was that, hour by hour, she began the process of turning the untidy rows into a neat and manicured vista. This wasn't for appearance sake. The canopy of leaves and fruit had to be just so. Fruit in the shade wasn't going to do much. Likewise, there was no point in having too many leaves creating moist conditions for mildew.

During a break, she headed off to the shops to get in a few supplies. On the way, she waved to Gus across the road – and then crossed to say hello.

"Can you believe it," she said. "No matter how much water we get to the vines, it's never enough."

"I hear you're doing a good job."

"Thanks Gus. Who's been spying on me? Ken?"

"Now you know me. I don't go in for gossip. I do like to hear of people putting a good effort into what they do though. I don't like lightweights, no matter what field they're in."

She liked Gus. He was one of the good guys. A presence in the village who got on with his work. No scandal. No trouble. A bit like herself these days.

"I'll bring you over a few bottles when we're done."

"Oh lovely. Gloria used to hand out bottles. I don't think she had the touch though."

"We're working with Kate Ramsey. She seems to know what she's doing."

"Ramsey's has a good reputation. Well done for

teaming up with them."

"I've got Ken to thank for that."

"Oh, mentioning Gloria… I heard Ed's having a clear-out."

"Who's Ed?"

"He cleared out Gloria's place. I just thought there might be a few items."

"What? Are you telling me Gloria's stuff is with some guy and nobody told me?"

"I doubt there's much left. Ed's place just gets a bit full so he has the occasional clear out of what he can't sell."

"Where is he?"

"He's the junk shop at the other end of the High Street. In fact, you won't see him until you go round by the last shop on the right."

Olivia marched through the village like cyborg storm-trooper. Bullets would have bounced off her. Ed didn't stand a chance.

"I'm Olivia Holmes," she announced on reaching his junk emporium. "I live at the Vines."

"I just need a couple of days' notice, love," he said. "Let me know when you're moving out and I can clear the place for you."

"Moving out? I'm part of the fabric of this village. I'm not going anywhere."

"You sound just like your aunt."

"She was my great aunt."

"Some would say she wasn't so great."

"Do you still have any of her belongings?"

"You timed that well. I'm just about to have a clear-out. Tell you what, you can have the whole lot for eighty quid."

"Eighty quid? To reclaim my own belongings? Gloria

left everything to me and my cousins. I can't believe you removed them from her home without permission."

"The funeral director said there was no interested family and suggested I clear out the rubbish. To be honest, it all looked like rubbish. I'll tell you what – fifty quid. Can't say fairer than that."

"I can see a court case in this. Theft is still on the statute books, you know. If you'll load it all up on your van and bring it round, we'll say no more about it."

"Thirty quid then. Call it storage tax."

"Done."

Ed brought Gloria's things round the following morning in a large van. Olivia was straight out the front, where Ed's co-worker, Dean, read from an inventory as Ed opened the back.

"One chest of drawers, one wardrobe, one sideboard…"

"Can I stop you a second," said Olivia. "When you cleared the place out, why did you leave a bed, a chair…?"

"Let me stop you there," said Ed. "We were working under difficult conditions. There was water pouring through the ceiling, so I said we should just take the best of a bad lot and get the hell out."

"You didn't try to fix it?"

"We were told a plumber was on the way. Turned out the plumber was Davy Knowles."

"Which meant he was on his way to the pub," said Dean.

Twenty minutes later, Ed and Dean had got everything back in and were enjoying a well-earned cup of tea.

"Be honest, what's this lot worth?" Olivia asked.

"Nothing and everything," said Ed. "I mean we sold the better stuff – a dining set, a cabinet… I couldn't have the rest of it blocking up my place forever."

"I'm surprised you didn't put the lot on eBay."

"We did," said Dean.

"It's unimportant dark furniture," said Ed. "People worry it's full of woodworm."

"It's not, is it?"

"No, but you still tend to get insulting bids."

"We did have one bloke in Ireland seem very keen," said Dean, "but it would have meant us spending half a lifetime getting it ready for international shipping to earn twenty-five quid."

Among the various items were some cardboard boxes. One of them had clothing. The other had personal items, including photos.

"We meant to send those up to that solicitor," said Ed, "but it all got forgotten."

After Ed and Dean had gone, Olivia took time to study framed photos of Gloria and Charlie on their wedding day and of Gloria's parents, Reginald and Hilda Whitman, probably taken in the 1920s. So Gloria's maiden name was Whitman. Then there was a batch of photos tied with string. One was of a couple wearing their finest in what had to be a studio, possibly Victorian. The man, standing, had a handlebar moustache, while the seated woman wore a bonnet. Then there were more old photos. Why didn't Gloria write the details on the back of them!

There were two more framed photos at the bottom. One of Charlie as a young man and one of Gloria, probably in her thirties. It was slightly cheeky as she was in a bathing suit. It was all very decent though. Not too much flesh on display, but you could see her curves. She was undoubtedly a good-looking woman. Confidant too. Olivia liked that.

She thought a few of them would look great on the wall. After all, didn't they put portraits up in Buckingham Palace and that other posh place – Raglington Hall?

The bathing suit photo though… it was quite a chunky wooden frame. Olivia thought it would look super-cool in a slim silver frame. She'd buy one. There was a nice shop in the village that might have just the thing.

Sue and Milo came down on the Saturday. They were amazed at the furniture. Whereas an unloved house full of dark wooden objects might appear depressing, these few items set against the walls Olivia had painted looked perfect.

"It's as if they belong," Milo joked.

There wasn't much time for discussing décor though. Once they'd enjoyed their coffee, it was out to the vines to carry on the never-ending tucking.

Olivia enjoyed the warm air and birdsong and felt completely immersed in the experience of running a vineyard. Anyone passing would have beheld experts, old hands – not three cousins hoping they weren't hindering grape growth.

"I'll tell you something," said Sue. "I'm getting to know our vines. It's like a classroom of children. Some more advanced than others, some more robust…"

"I've heard you talking to them," said Milo. "You'll be giving them names next."

"Ooh, good idea," said Sue.

Olivia couldn't tell whether she was joking or not.

"Do you talk to them?" Milo asked Olivia.

"Now you mention it, I think I do."

"Don't you just love days like these?" said Sue.

"I do," said Olivia. "I really feel part of it."

"Me too," said Milo. "I feel like an army captain inspecting the troops."

Olivia chuckled. The rows did look a bit military, especially now most of them had endured a regulation haircut. But she loved the connection to the process of plants growing under the sun. She loved having a role. That meant during her off-duty moments, her pleasure at everything going on was intensified. Just strolling along a row to take in how the plants were developing, if they were healthy, what needed to be done… she had never experienced anything like it. Working at Prior Grove had been like dipping a toe in the sea. This was diving in head-first.

And, of course, it all looked so romantic. This wasn't just a vineyard, it was part of the Kentish quilt of fields, hedges, woods and villages. It was a part of the green under the blue and they were all bonded to it all. They were becoming country folk. At least, Olivia felt she was.

"Do you think we've found our place in the world," she asked.

"Possibly," said Sue. "We shall have to wait and see."

"Milo?"

"Maybe. Who knows. I still love the city life."

Maybe Sue and Milo were still townies at heart. Maybe Olivia herself was too. Maybe this was just an extended working holiday. Perhaps she would tire of it. It was hard work, after all. But she couldn't think negatively on a day such as this. It was too beautiful.

"Barbecue and beers later?" Milo suggested.

Olivia smiled. Yes, the glorious countryside, barbecue, beers, and family.

"I'll sort that out," she said. And so, during their next

break, she took the car to the High Street to get supplies from the Kelvin's the butcher, Shore's the greengrocer, and Village Wines for beers and prosecco. She also popped in the homewares shop to buy the perfect silver frame for Gloria's photo.

The following morning, Olivia awoke with a heavy heart. The barbecue had gone well. Now Milo was snoring in the next room, while Sue was at Cam's, no doubt curled up with him – lucky girl.

For Olivia, it was the anniversary of her greatest loss. Not Alistair, but her unborn baby.

With Milo still asleep, she went out among the vines to commune with nature. Life was abundant and all around her. But, for a moment, she felt separate. Lonely. The countryside was a big place. And loss and ongoing grief could freeze a person.

Would it always be like this? She knew it would. If she ever got into a relationship, she'd probably have to make an excuse to have a day away each year. Unless she found someone she could share it with. Imagine that? A partner she could share thoughts of Jamie with. It wouldn't happen, of course. That level of trust was way beyond what she could bestow on any human.

After breakfast she waved Milo off. It was back to normal.

"Just you and me, Gloria. Ooh, your new frame."

She opened the old wooden frame to remove the photo – only, there was a folded sheet of paper behind the picture.

Olivia took it out and unfolded it. It was a letter.

'My dearest Gloria,

I'll be away from you for a time now, and I can only say how sad that makes me feel. I know you feel the same way, but I hope the memories of our 'moments' will keep you warm in the long winter nights.'

Olivia stopped reading.

Ken, you old rascal. Well, young rascal at the time, I suppose...

She wasn't sure if to read on. It was a private matter. And Ken wouldn't be happy to learn that his words of love were being pored over by an outsider.

That said, curiosity is an unstoppable force.

'It will be at least six months until I can get back to Kent, so do get yourself involved in plenty of village activities to while away the time. Christmas should certainly be busy enough to take your mind off my arms being around your beautiful body while my lips caress you all over. I'll be busy too, so that's good.

Looking forward to our eventual reunion.

Until then,
All my love
Raymond'

What??? Raymond? Not Ken?

"Gloria? What have you been up to? You and Ray? You kept that quiet. First Ken, then Ray. I'm going to shorten the legs on that pedestal you put yourself on so our eyes are at least level."

And then she softened.

"I hope you found some happiness with Ray. It

sounds like you did. I promise I won't tell Ken. He really loved you though. You wouldn't have gone wrong there. This Ray must have been quite a catch though."

She smiled as she hid the letter in its new frame. Then it was just a matter of hanging the photo on the wall.

"Eat your hearts out, you lords and ladies, you kings and queens. This is the Vines, and the people here count for something."

27

Hot August

As the weeks passed, temperatures rose, and the small, hard, green grapes grew to reach half their final size. From here on in, they would begin to ripen – the stage known as veraison – and swell and soften as their sugars – glucose and fructose – increased.

Olivia watched with wonder.

"You see that?" said Ken. "The outer clusters? They're advancing faster than those in the shade by the trunk."

"I'm understanding it a little better," said Olivia. "The vine is a mother, biologically programmed to feed all resources into the grapes and their seeds. That's the next generation. If water and nutrients are short, the vine makes sacrifices to ensure her children don't die."

"You think of the vine as female?"

She bent down to stroke Beano. "Viv does. And so do I."

"Well, I don't like to see cruelty to women, but vineyard owners sometimes hold back water just to encourage early ripening."

"Yes, well, I don't think of them as women when I'm being cruel to them."

There was a distant rumble. At first, Olivia thought it might be thunder, but no – it was single source, a rumbling, thrumming noise…

A World War Two plane thundered over.

Beano looked scared so Olivia picked him up.

"Must be going to an air show," said Ken, his voice raised to be heard.

But Olivia was transported. She could imagine Ray and Gloria under an apple tree, the plane flying over, war in the balance, nothing to lose, everything to gain… and Ken and Gloria… and Charlie and Gloria… because who knew how the War would turn out?

Olivia, Ken and Beano continued their stroll through the vineyard, down one alley, back along the next, up and down, checking and enjoying the sun. The vine canes were beginning the process of turning from green and supple to brown and hard.

High above, not a plane now but a swift. Or a swallow. She asked Ken if there was a way to tell the difference.

"Don't bother," he told her. "We'll probably confuse both with a house martin or a sand martin."

She wanted to ask him about Gloria and Ray. But she couldn't.

And then her phone rang. It was Alistair.

"Me and Beano were heading off anyway," said Ken. "We'll see ourselves out."

"See you later then."

Olivia answered Alistair's call.

"Hi Liv. Um… just thought you should know Steph and me… we're getting married."

She almost dropped the phone. Her next response was

to feel the urge to swear, but the retreating Ken and Beano were still within earshot.

"You're getting married?" she eventually managed to say. "I hope this isn't a bloody invite."

"No, just a courtesy call. I didn't want you to hear it from someone else. I thought you deserved better."

"You thought I deserved better? How bloody gallant of you."

"Well, now you know. The baby's due soon, so… anyway, I hope things are going well for you and Gerry. I never had him down as a country gent. Bye Liv."

He ended the call but Olivia couldn't stop staring at the phone. That would be the last time she ever spoke to him. The very last time. A milestone had been passed. The last one, in fact.

She called him back.

"Liv? You okay?"

"Alistair… look… I hope everything goes well with the wedding and the baby. You'll make a great dad. I always knew it. I could just never persuade you, could I. Seriously, my very, very best wishes to you and Stephanie. I hope everything goes well."

"Thanks, Liv. That means a lot."

"For the record, I'm not with Gerry anymore. I'm trying to find my own place in the world. No time for men."

"Right, well, I hope you find what you want. You deserve to be happy. The very best of luck, Liv."

"And you. Bye."

She ended the call. Of all the things she might have said, wishing Alistair well felt just fine.

*

August in the vineyard meant more repetitive work. Tucking up seemed to be a never-ending round of trimming the tops and removing side shoots. Good canopy management wasn't just about maximizing this year's crop, but next year's too, because those vital kick-starting buds for next year were already forming inside this year's canes.

It was during this time that Olivia noticed something off about some of the grapes. While the chardonnay was performing well, with healthy-looking bunches, the pinot noir had a distinctly odd look, with some berries full and others still tiny. Was some hideous disease about to destroy them?

She went online to discover what was happening. It gave her cause for concern, so she called in on Ken.

"Rain, did it?" he asked.

"Recently? No, the weather's been lovely. You know that, Ken."

"No, I mean did it rain during pollination? I don't mean a drizzle. I mean a bloody great big downpour."

Olivia's mind drifted back to more than one big downpour.

"Let's go and look at everything, shall we?" he suggested, getting Beano's leash.

Among the vines, Ken delivered his opinion.

"I've seen worse," he said. "The rain came as the fruit was setting. The chardonnay was done, so you're okay there. Your pinot noir though... pumpkins and peas."

"Yes, that's what it said online."

"Pumpkins and peas, hens and chicks – some are small and won't develop because the rain washed away too much pollen. It's not a disaster, but it will affect output."

"Right... well... I'd better make us a cup of tea then."

A short while later, they sat on chairs on the patio

drinking their tea. Olivia had put down a bowl of water for Beano and she laughed at the mess he made splashing his tongue in it.

"I noticed the photographs on the wall," Ken said.

"Yes, they were about to be thrown out by Ed and Dean. I only found out the other day they had some of Gloria's stuff."

"They look very nice, Olivia. Very nice…"

"You must miss her."

"I do. We were meant for each other but life had other ideas."

"Charlie died a fair while back. Didn't you think of getting together with Gloria after a decent interval?"

"I tried, but she didn't want it. I put that down to her pain at losing Charlie. I kept my distance after that."

Tricky.

"Did she become good friends with Raymond?"

"That was just a work relationship."

"I thought she'd known him since her teen years."

"She would have told me had anything developed between them. Why, what have you heard?"

"Me? Nothing. Gloria's reputation is a good one. Rock solid."

"Yes, well, as far as I'm concerned, Ray took advantage. That Kirncroft's winery? They couldn't make lemonade. All I'll say is the stories of Ray having the grapes under-weighed so he could split the profit with a mate of his who worked there… well… I won't speak ill of the dead."

"No. Absolutely."

On a Saturday at the very end of August, Olivia, Sue and Milo took up an invite to Ramsey's. Kate, Elsa and Jack wanted opinions about potential sugar balance for a sparkling rosé. Archie the winemaker had come over from Canterbury, which made Olivia feel a little out of place, but the conviviality of the occasion soon dispensed with that.

Various bottles were labelled with their sugar dosage and this was an opportunity to see how they had matured so far.

"This is what it's all about," said Jack.

"This and strolling along the alleys in summer," said Elsa.

Archie, Jack and Elsa popped the corks of half a dozen bottles, and the wine fizzed and foamed. Olivia felt the excitement rising. This was a big moment for Ramsey's as a wine supplier. They'd had that little tasting session earlier in the year, but this seemed more formal. She knew all too well the kind of work that would have gone into producing these grapes the year before last. It was also a possible taste of her own future. She could see it now. Their first vintage, ready to test and balance.

Olivia accepted a glass of Bottle 3 fizz.

"Ah yes, good old Bottle 3."

Archie explained the aim. Not to try to think like an expert, but as someone who enjoyed sparkling wine. Simple questions were the order of the day. Was a bottle with a little extra sugar bringing the best out of the grapes while remaining in the dry range? Balance was everything.

Olivia examined her wine. It had a lovely sparkle.

"Okay," Archie continued. "We're looking for a nice collar around the glass. We're looking for a steady bubble train rising up through the wine. We're looking for the bubbles to be small."

Olivia checked all those requirements.

"Now we're taking in the bouquet... let those aromas

linger…"

Olivia enjoyed the fruity waft hitting her nostrils. The only disappointment was the wine being at room temperature. She understood the reason for that – coldness would mask some of the sugar taste.

"And sip…"

Olivia's wine tasted perfect. Although she guessed Archie wouldn't describe it as such.

Everyone had to jot down their observations. Luckily, Archie had handed round printed checklists, so it was just a matter of ticking boxes rather than writing a short essay.

Once she had got through all six, Olivia could see how a pinch of sugar more or less per bottle could make a difference. She still felt Bottle 3 was a winner though, balanced, with enough acidity to enhance the fruit.

Once they had finished, Archie took in the results while everyone else chatted about winemaking and weather and sipped a chilled glass of an established sparkling white. That with fresh sandwiches made a perfect lunch.

Then Archie declared a preference for the Bottle 3 dosage and was glad to see overwhelming approval for it.

The following day, they popped over to taste the wines again direct from the fridge. Bottle 3 remained a winner, but Olivia was taken with the way she liked the drier wine much more now that it was cold.

Elsa and Jack were very pleased. The remaining test bottles would stay on lees until February, when the whole dosage taste trial would happen again before they made a final choice.

It was followed by another perfect lunch.

*

Later, as Milo drove them back to the Vines, he had some news.

"I've got an interview on Friday. Possible new job with another law firm."

"Ooh," said Sue. "Sounds exciting."

"It's one of those informal interviews – a lunch and chat thing. It could take me to New York."

"The lunch?" said Sue.

"No, the job."

"Oh. How long for?"

"I'm not sure yet, but it would be a big boost to my career. I'd be giving advice to wealthy corporations looking to branch into the UK."

"Best of luck with it, Milo," said Olivia. "I'm sure you'll get it."

An hour later, Olivia and Sue were waving their cousin off.

"I think that's him done," said Sue as Milo's car disappeared up the lane.

Olivia felt a little down.

"It was the three musketeers. All for one and one for all."

But now it was something less.

28

September Sun

The first few days of September were glorious. Summer had no intention of packing up early. The skies were blue, the fields were green, and the weather forecast was for warm air coming up from North Africa. Olivia and Sue stripped leaves to expose more fruit to the ever lower sun and felt a rising sense of destiny heading their way.

The vineyard year was almost complete.

Thanks to advice from Viv and Ken, they knew it wasn't sensible to set a specific date for harvest, so they were looking at the beginning of October as a rough target. The grapes would be ready in their own good time, depending on the weather. As to exactly when, Olivia and Sue would have to take a deep breath and say go. Even seasoned vineyard owners would be worrying about getting it wrong.

"I wish Milo were here," said Sue.

Olivia agreed. "I suppose I thought we might stay close as a family."

"Me too."

Sue continued with her work, exposing more of the fruit to the available light. But only for a moment.

"It just occurred to me," she said. "We're not any old family. We're the Holmes-Bridge-Corbett family and that means something."

Olivia lowered her secateurs. Sue was right.

Friday morning meant a drive up to London for Olivia. There, she used the car park at the Barbican and met Sue outside the theatre. Being something of a spy, Sue had obtained the address simply by asking Milo if his potential new employer would be taking him to a good restaurant. Now it was just a short walk there to put things right.

They were outside ten minutes before the twelve-thirty meeting, waiting, poised…

A couple of minutes beforehand, they spotted the target approaching with a smartly-dressed, middle-aged woman.

"Here we go," said Sue.

Olivia joined her cousin in unfurling their home-made banners.

Sue's carried a well-crafted painting of a bottle along with a proclamation: 'Ask for Milo's Choice English Wine!'

Olivia's stated, 'It's A Family Thing'.

The following Sunday was Olivia's forty-fifth birthday. Sue baked a cake and they opened a bottle of sparkling Ramsey's pink.

"Happy birthday, cousin," said Sue, clinking glasses.

"Thanks for the cake and the wine, Sue. And for everything. All the support. All the friendship."

"You'll make me blush at this rate."

It would have been nice to get Cass down, but her old friend had dodged two invites. Maybe life was moving on. Or maybe she'd come down another time.

"When's your birthday, Sue?"

"January. I never mentioned it. Perhaps I should have."

"We'll make up for it next time."

"I wonder how Milo's doing in New York."

"Well, it's just a short pleasure trip to… what did he say – scope it out."

But Sue sighed. "I think we've lost him."

Outside, the September sun had gone. It was still mild, but now they had low heavy cloud with a liking for spitting and drizzling. Later, when Ken and Beano popped round, they peered out of the back door toward the vines.

"Fingers crossed," said Ken. "You've worked too hard to lose it all now."

"Amen to that," said Sue. "I was reading up on botrytis."

"I'm sure we'll be alright," said Olivia, attempting to head off any negativity.

"Dull days, damp atmosphere," said Ken. "You can't rule anything out. A couple of years back, Ramsey's lost a lot of their pinot gris to it."

Olivia had also read up on botrytis, the grim fruit fungus. It liked the kind of moist weather and mild temperatures they were currently experiencing in Kent, and it was uniformly ranked by winegrowers as their worst nightmare.

"The question is," said Ken, "are you going to spray?"

"Yes," was the definite response.

The following day, she addressed the vines and grapes.

"Now listen, I'm no fan of chemical warfare, but this is serious. There's a scary fungus coming to get you, so I'm going to zap you with some horrible compounds. It's for your own good, so no complaining."

And so spraying commenced. One time around as an initial measure with a second spray to follow before the end of the month. Hopefully, that would be close enough to harvest to keep the grapes safe without rendering them unfit for human consumption.

A few days later, with brighter weather returning, Olivia took the opportunity to borrow a ladder from Gus to paint the window frames – not just to freshen the place up, but give them some protection before another winter added to their woes.

While she was up there, she thought to repaint the fading sign that just about proclaimed 'The Vines'. Only, now she was up close, she could see the slight indentations of the original lettering. Almost eroded by wind and rain, it was difficult to work out what it spelled... but it seemed to be 'Whitman Farm 1962'.

No... not 1962. That's an 8 not a 9.

'Whitman Farm 1862.'

Wasn't Whitman Gloria's maiden name?

Olivia came down from the ladder and made herself a cup of thought-stirring tea. If Gloria's family name was Whitman, and the sign stating 'The Vines' was Charlie's doing, then they most likely bought the house from the Whitman family – Gloria's family. Or maybe they inherited it. Whichever, the Whitmans clearly had a long association with the house and the village.

Hang on... Gloria's dad was also my gran's dad. My great grandad, in fact.

"Oh my God…"

She put her tea down and made her way round to the High Street. She tried eleven shops without success. Then she tried Shore's the greengrocers. There she asked Theresa Shore if she knew anything of the Whitman family.

"No, but Mum might."

She summoned her elderly mother, Judy from the back room.

"Yes, I recall the name. There was Gloria, Veronica and Katherine, who I think called herself Kitty."

"That was them, yes. Kitty was my gran."

"Oh well, you'll know more about them than I do."

"That's the thing. I don't. I never knew much about my family until recently."

"I see. Well, the Whitmans were hereabouts when I was young."

"Gloria's parents were Reginald and Hilda Whitman, if that helps."

"Yes, I remember Reg and Hilda. Yes. And I recall Reg's dad, Henry. And there was the grandad… what was his name. George? Yes, George. He was quite old when I was a girl, but I remember his handlebar moustache. I'd imagine he was the one who had the house built. There was bit of money in the family, see. Not with Gloria and her sisters, but way back. Have you looked at the panel in the Old Hall?"

"Yes, but…"

"I'm sure there are Whitmans on it."

"Whitmans? You mean…?"

"Your family's been here four hundred years, my love. This is your home."

Olivia was overcome. She raced around to the Old Hall, where a couple of late-season tourists were taking photos.

"Sorry, just need to check somethi…"

And there they were, below Robert May, among a dozen lesser names recorded as contributors to the hall's construction – Josiah and Jeremiah Whitman.

"My great-great-great-great-great-great…" But she couldn't work out how many greats it would be.

She was beside herself. Not only was she the great-great-great granddaughter of the man who built the house at Whitman Farm in 1862, she could now look down at her feet standing on the very same spot as her ancestors four centuries earlier.

Three words escaped her lips.

"I belong here."

29

First Harvest

It was the very end of September and Olivia and Ken were in the vineyard, tasting the grapes.

"Good sugar level," said Ken, trying a noir.

"The acidity is definitely dropping," said Olivia. She had tasted from the vine a few days earlier.

Ken broke open another grape.

"Good seeds."

Olivia made a note in her little book. Vineyard Viv had been adamant. You could sing and dance all you like – but you *had* to record the date, weight, hue, number of seeds, texture and taste, sugar and acidity and any visible faults. This was how you became an expert – by understanding everything going on, every year, to build knowledge of what works and what doesn't.

"An extra week for the chardonnay?" Ken suggested.

Olivia agreed. Based on progress so far, that would be a good harvest time.

"And as soon as possible for the pinots?" she suggested.

Ken nodded. "Some years, it's the other way round. Nature's funny like that."

Olivia was happy. The noir, Meunier and gris had all ripened nicely. As for the older vines – the Reichensteiner, Müller-Thurgau, Schönburger, Huxelrebe, Ortega and Dornfelder – they could be split into two harvests.

That meant two picking dates. Fortunately, they had already picked the pickers. Olivia, Ken, Sue, Annie, Cam, Ed and Dean, both Ramsey daughters, and even Jo the solicitor had been roped in. The picking crates were ready, the wheelbarrows were ready, two vans had been hired, and the time was fast approaching. There was just one more person Olivia wanted to get involved.

"We're paying everyone in future wine," she told Gus at the petrol station. "It'll be a quality fizz."

Gus had been working on a Fiat's brakes in the garage but had spotted her crossing the road. Now he was leaning against the door frame cleaning his hands with a cloth.

He seemed to be weighing her offer.

"We've done quite well, I think," she said. "Obviously we never had the benefit of Ray, but we've managed to cobble together enough expert advice."

"Well, you've done alright with Milly's advice," he said. "At least I assume that's where you've been getting it from."

"Milly? Who's Milly?"

"My advice is get as many sensible people as you can muster. All you want to concentrate on now is picking all the grapes and getting them to the winery."

"Gus? I said who's Milly?"

"Milly Ramsey."

"One of the Ramseys from Terry Ramsey's vineyard and winery?"

"Milly's husband was Dan Ramsey, brother of Terry, whose wife Kate is the wine manager there. They all know their stuff. I assumed that's why Ken recommended their place to you."

"Milly Ramsey. I suppose I could drive over there."

"Drive? Milly lives down Frampton Lane."

"Frampton Lane? You mean *this* Frampton Lane?"

She was indicating the lane that ran down from the main road alongside the petrol station.

"Last house on the right," said Gus. "I'm surprised Ken never mentioned her."

Back at the Vines, Olivia was trying to get her head around the latest developments in Ken's hidden life when Sue came along from Cam's.

"Well, the vines did their thing in spite of us then," she said.

"Yes…"

Olivia's phone rang. It was a familiar name on the screen, so she put in on loudspeaker.

"Hi Liv, it's Milo."

"Hello Milo," she and Sue trilled.

"I'm not going to New York. I'm staying in England."

Sue's squeals almost deafened Olivia.

"Milo, if you have any free time," Olivia managed to say, "we have two harvests coming up – one of them tomorrow."

"I'll be there," said Milo. "Actually, I'm over here."

A car horn sounded from thirty yards up the lane.

Milo had returned. And he was soon in their embrace.

"I couldn't leave the Vines behind," he said.

"I'll have to stop you there," said Olivia. "We've all left the Vines behind."

She pointed to the sign high up on the wall. It was easy to read now that it had been carefully repainted with black lettering on a cream background.

Whitman Farm 1862.

"We'll explain it over a cup of tea," said Sue.

Five minutes later, Milo was blown away by the onrush of family history. But Olivia and Sue were just as overwhelmed by Milo's commitment to them, his family.

"I actually had two interviews," he told them. "I wanted to feel where I needed to be. That's why the other one was to join a firm in Kent as an associate."

"And that's the job you took?"

"It's a long way from London, but it's a brilliant firm. They... *we* have two offices, one in Kent and one in Sussex. I'll be based in Canterbury."

Olivia was overjoyed. From Maybrook, Canterbury was twenty miles deeper into Kent and would be easy to reach by car.

"What about accommodation?" Sue asked.

"You could stay here and commute," said Olivia. "You're still an owner and I don't expect it would take that long to get there."

"I've already done the research. I'll be renting a flat for the first few months, then I'll look into buying somewhere once I've settled in."

"Um... hate to intrude," said Sue, "but what does Jaz think of Canterbury?"

"She wanted me to take the New York job, which I understand. She's not too keen on Kent, so she said she'd think about it."

"Right," said Olivia. That didn't sound too good.

"Lots of history there," said Sue.

"Yes," said Milo. "I've been googling like mad. It's a cathedral city and was a pilgrimage site in the Middle Ages. I've had a good few walks around it. There's Roman stuff there, cobbled streets, timber-framed houses… real picture postcard stuff."

Olivia decided they needed fizz to celebrate Milo's return, so she set of for the village to get a bottle.

Leaving the house, she spotted Ken and Beano way up ahead. She thought to call out but guessed she'd probably catch them fairly quickly.

As it was, by the time she was drawing near, they were crossing the road. Olivia stopped and watched them trundle down Frampton Lane. No doubt on route for the last house on the right.

The cheeky old so-and-so.

That night, as Milo headed for bed, Olivia made her and Sue hot chocolate drinks.

"Cam says his brother's looking to retire in three or four years."

"Oh?"

"Well, they have no children."

"And?"

"Well, they've got that huge field that backs onto ours. Five acres, give or take."

"Oh, you mean…a land grab."

"I think they'd want paying."

"Well, it's something to think about."

Olivia sipped her drink.

"You don't have to stay over, Sue. You could stay with Cam."

"Certainly not. This is a time for solidarity."

"Fair enough."

"Besides, I'm working up my courage."

"For what? I thought you and he were already…"

"I'm going to ask him to marry me."

"Oh. Right. I see. Well, that's brilliant."

"Do you think he'll say yes?"

"He'd be a right twit to say no, Sue. You and Cam are like Ginger Rogers and Fred Astaire."

"We don't dance, Olivia."

"Figuratively speaking. You're a perfect match, Sue. Of course he'll say yes. And you should dance."

Olivia showed her Vineyard Viv's latest post. A short video dedicated to Dionysus…

"…yes, the god of the grape harvest, winemaking and wine," said Viv, seemingly bursting out of the small screen on Olivia's phone. "Also the god of fertility, theatre and religious ecstasy. If that doesn't inspire a little pre-harvest dance, I don't know what will."

Viv danced.

Holding the phone up and copying, Olivia danced too.

Sue? She laughed. And then she danced.

The following morning, they were up early. Too early, in fact. It was four a.m., and their first helpers weren't due until six.

"I couldn't sleep," said Sue.

"Me neither," said Milo.

"I could sleep," said Olivia, "but I kept dreaming about tidal waves washing away the vines, earthquakes destroying the vines, asteroids from space… you get the idea."

Cam was first to call – at ten to six. Then came Ken and Beano, Annie from the pub, Jo the solicitor, and, striding down the lane…

"Gus!"

"I thought some extra hands might be useful."

He was with Harpo and Killy – minus their accordion and guitar.

What a cold, damp morning they had chosen, but Olivia felt nothing but warmth. This was a big, big, big day.

Out in the vineyard, the team plus a dog got started at the far end – Olivia reckoning that working their way back to the house would give them a sense of progress.

"These don't seem too good," called Sue almost immediately.

Olivia and Milo raced over to be confronted by a pinot noir vine bearing fruit tainted by grey rot.

"How the..?" Sue was distraught.

"Leave that one," said Olivia. "Just move on."

Olivia returned to her own row. Everything had been perfect. They were good for sugars, low acidity, tannins, everything. And now they had rot.

"Chin up," said Ken. "Everyone gets a little rot from time to time."

They picked as fast as they could, with crates mounted on wheelbarrows moving to and fro, and being loaded onto the vans. Then Olivia and Gus drove the bounty to Ramsey's, where they unloaded and had their fruit weighed.

Kate oversaw the grapes being pressed, which meant Olivia and Gus could wash out the crates and get back to picking.

At Whitman Farm, it was everyone picking, packing and hauling down to the vans. Ken and Beano were excused by now – exhausted. So was Annie.

The second batch soon went to Ramsey's. As did

subsequent batches – until many tons of grapes were ready for life in tanks and barrels.

At the end of the day, Ken and Annie were summoned to Whitman Farm to rejoin them for bacon sandwiches, cheese toasties, and beer and wine all round.

They had done it.

Enjoying the calm, Sue was by the back door. Olivia joined her.

"What a day, Sue. I've never had one like that before."

"No, a special day. Very much so."

Olivia traced Sue's gaze to the biggest of the outbuildings. Cam was storing away the crates for their upcoming second harvest.

She nudged Sue.

"Go on."

"What now?"

"Why not?"

"Wish me luck."

Sue went up through the garden and veered to the right where Cam was emerging from the building. Olivia watched them. She couldn't hear, which was right and proper. But she couldn't look away either. Sue was possibly asking Cam to marry her. It was like a silent film.

Is it going well? What's he doing? Oh, they're hugging. That's always a good sign.

Sue returned, saying nothing.

She brushed away a tear.

Olivia was about to go off like a volcano. "Well???"

Sue nodded. Then they both hugged and cried.

In the midst of their embrace, Gus tapped Olivia on the shoulder.

"If you need me again, just shout."

Cam came in and Sue took the opportunity to share the news. The cheer would have been heard in the High

Street. While congratulations went on, Olivia stepped out into the garden to take in the air.

"Well, Gloria, we've achieved quite a bit so far, wouldn't you say?"

Ken and Beano came out to join her.

"Ken, have you ever made mistakes in love, tried to put it right and got that wrong too?"

"We're human. We're always making mistakes. It shouldn't stop us trying though."

"I thought Alistair was the love of my life. I was wrong. Then I thought it might be Gerry, and I was very wrong. Then Leo came along and I kind of lost my mind… well, at least my focus. What do you think of Gus?"

"Gus is the salt of this earth, Olivia."

"He told me about Milly Ramsey."

"Did he? The rat."

"Why did you never mention Milly?"

"Oh well… I suppose there was enough gossip doing the rounds. I reckon we're entitled to a little privacy, don't you?"

"So, Gloria *wasn't* the love of your life."

"On the contrary, she *was*… and then she wasn't. I thought, what the hell, I'm not throwing my life away. Milly's a wonderful woman. Taught me everything I know about many things. Grapes among them. Although, with us, that wasn't the most important thing."

"Is it always like this in deepest Kent?"

"No, Olivia, this is the sleepy old countryside. Nothing much happens here."

30

Second Harvest

On a beautiful day, with the countryside turning from green to gold, the picking team gathered again to bring in the chardonnay and the remainder of the older varieties. Olivia was so pleased to see them all, but reserved a sympathetic smile for poor old Ken and Beano. This surely had to be their last harvest.

In the bright, early morning sun, they set to it.

The chardonnay had benefitted from its extra time on the vine. No longer green, it bore a golden hue that hopefully indicated a sweet fruit with the ideal balance of sugar and acid. Just the thing for a classic sparkling wine.

They worked fast but with care, snipping each bunch while supporting it with their free hand. Slowly, the grapes were laid into the crates, and slowly the number of picked bunches grew.

Everyone took to tasting grapes as they went and there was general approval.

*

At Ramsey's, Olivia and Gus were greeted by Milly Ramsey.

"You've done ever so well, Olivia. I'll inform Jo you're on track to meet the conditions of the will. You'll have no trouble producing a bottle of fizz from that lot. Congratulations."

The rest of the Ramseys came out to congratulate Olivia. It wasn't long before she was texting Sue and Milo to share the good news and reveal that Milly, Ken and Beano had been Jo the solicitor's spies.

Amid the hullaballoo, Olivia spotted a woman with Kate Ramsey, bringing in grapes, and looking familiar…

Olivia caught her attention.

"Viv?"

"Hello?"

"Vineyard Viv – you're my hero. I've done all your dances."

"Haha – well there's another one to do later. When I've completed the harvest. Make sure you join me… er…?"

"It's Olivia. Liv, if you like."

"Liv and Viv. We could be a double act. Perhaps you could be in my next vlog?"

"Me? Seriously?"

"Yes, you, seriously."

"Wow, fame at last!"

"You're not kidding. We get at least two hundred views a month."

Viv, Olivia discovered, lived in a village three miles from Maybrook. The two of them vowed to meet up and swap notes.

Driving back to Whitman Farm, Gus was in the leading van. Around halfway home, he pulled over. Fearing he might have engine trouble or a puncture,

Olivia pulled in behind him.

"Everything alright, Gus?" she asked on reaching his open window.

"You're the real deal, Olivia. Full of commitment, full of hard work, and so full of passion it's practically pouring out of you. Don't tell me I'm wrong because I'm a good judge of people."

"Are you suggesting we see more of each other?"

"I am. You're someone I can trust."

"There's seems to be a van door between us."

"We can still kiss through the window," he pointed out.

"You're right. So we can."

During the weeks that followed, they set out their aims for Whitman Farm. Milo saw it as a long-term investment. In fact, he'd started to see it that way a while back, which is why he had dragged out his efforts to raise any buy-out money – on the basis he didn't want to lose Olivia. Likewise, Sue wanted to stay in, albeit while living next door. Her only concern was that they should have an owner named Olivia on site, someone who knew their vines and who was passionate about the whole business. English sparkling wine was on the rise and she wanted them to be a part of it.

So, during those same weeks, the trip to Ramsey's became a regular run. Fermentation was taking place and they wanted to be on top of the situation. Olivia wanted to become an expert on every aspect of wine.

She made sure she tasted as often as possible, from grape juice to the fermented liquid, to the proto-wine going into tanks or barrels. She wanted to get to know the wine's personality, like you might a growing child.

It had been quite a year. From pruning in the freezing cold to, hopefully, discovering her place in the world. In fact, her only dealings with her old life in London would be related to putting her apartment up for sale.

Taste-wise, all was good. The pinot noir had been a little down in terms of quantity, but they had avoided the major kill factors: a frost while the sap is rising, super-heavy rain while the vines are self-pollinating, a poor summer that restricts growth, and botrytis that can wipe out a crop just before harvest.

Olivia had learned much and it made her smile. Maybe she was adept at this kind of life. Or maybe the land was simply a good teacher.

Next year, she wanted to learn more about nutrition, disease control, and canopy management – and a range of dances to cover all situations.

By November, the alleys had been mown, the weeds dealt with, and there was some tying to do before winter came a-howling. Soon the first frost would strip all remaining leaves. The vines would become dormant. That would give Olivia and Gus time to have meals with Cam and Sue, and to get over to see Milo and his new girlfriend – who Olivia was dying to meet.

Olivia would never forget a single moment of the year now sliding away into memory. The season was done, Christmas wasn't far off, and, at Ramsey's, their wine was ticking over nicely in its own good time.

A bottle of fizz for Jo to seal the deal? To win their inheritance? They knew they could knock out one of those in treble-quick time.

And they would. To secure the deeds. After all, they weren't daft.

But their proper first wine? They wouldn't be rushing it. This was a genuine business now. Olivia would bring in hired hands to help when she needed it. She would study. She would learn. And she would be buoyed by the presence of Gloria and Jamie, Sue and Milo, and Viv and Gus.

From the lounge window at Whitman Farm, the former office worker peered out over a chilly, moonlit landscape and wondered what next year would bring. She already had plans for replanting some of the older vines. And then there was Charlie's nature reserve. There was a lot to do on a vineyard – far more than she could have ever imagined. Another cold winter of pruning? Wrapped up with scarves and proper wellies? For Olivia Holmes, it couldn't come around fast enough.

The End

Thank you so much for choosing *Olivia Holmes Has Inherited A Vineyard*. I hope you enjoyed reading it as much as I enjoyed writing it. If so, you might be interested in my other books. Written in a similar style are:

Those Lazy, Hazy, Crazy Days of Summer

and

The Patron of Lost Causes

For more information, simply pop over to my website:

www.markdaydy.co.uk